"Don't you care about anything but what you *want?*"

"There are certain emotions that tend to take precedence over others in all of us. Do you think me incapable of recognizing desire in a woman? You vibrate with it whenever I touch you."

"I think you've misunderstood me," she began haltingly. "I'm not what I might have seemed to be."

"You claimed to enjoy sexual relationships without censure," Alexis quoted. "I grant you that right. I think it's time I showed you how the Greeks make love to a woman."

Dear Reader,

We know from your letters that many of you enjoy traveling to foreign locations—especially from the comfort of your favorite chair. Well, sit back, put your feet up and let Harlequin Presents take you on a year-long tour of Europe. **Postcards from Europe** will feature a special title every month set in one of your favorite European countries, written by one of your favorite Harlequin Presents authors. We begin our exciting journey in Greece, so enjoy the sunshine, the ancient sites and the warm hospitality of this glorious corner of Europe. And revel in an exciting romance, too!

The Editors

P.S. Don't miss the fascinating facts we've compiled about Greece. You'll find them at the end of the story.

KAY THORPE

The Alpha Man

Harlequin Books

TORONTO • NEW YORK • LONDON
AMSTERDAM • PARIS • SYDNEY • HAMBURG
STOCKHOLM • ATHENS • TOKYO • MILAN
MADRID • WARSAW • BUDAPEST • AUCKLAND

ISBN 0-373-11619-5

THE ALPHA MAN

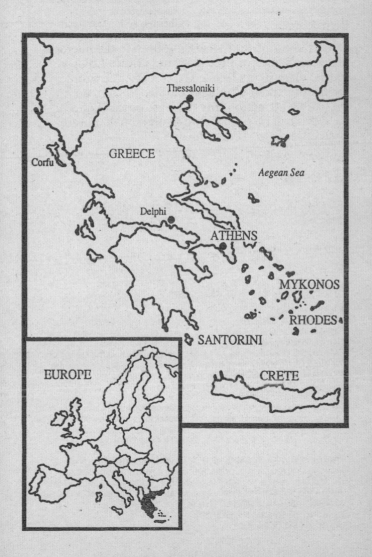

Dear Reader,

Of all the countries I've visited, both in the interests
of research and for pure pleasure, Greece holds a
special place in my heart. The scenery, the people,
the history and mythology combine to form an
irresistible attraction. My feelings for this Land of
the Gods can be summed up in one simple phrase:
Greece, *s'agapo*—I love you!

Enjoy!

Kay Thorpe

Books by Kay Thorpe

HARLEQUIN PRESENTS

1446—NIGHT OF ERROR
1501—TROUBLE ON TOUR
1534—LASTING LEGACY
1556—WILD STREAK
1571—LEFT IN TRUST
1603—PAST ALL REASON

HARLEQUIN ROMANCE

2151—TIMBER BOSS
2232—THE WILDERNESS TRAIL
2234—FULL CIRCLE

CHAPTER ONE

THIS, thought Zoe, feeling the sun caressing her whole body as she reclined her chair to its full extent, was pure bliss! She could summon some very real sympathy for those back home in England suffering a particularly cold and wet spring. Here, in southern Greece, the weather had been good for several weeks, the temperatures rising daily. Another month, and it would probably be too hot to lie out unshielded at this hour of the afternoon.

The shower of water droplets hitting her heated skin drew a smothered yelp to her lips. Sitting up again, she shook a mock fist at the girl clinging to the edge of the swimming-pool bare feet away.

'I'll get you for that!' she threatened. 'You just wait!'

The other laughed back, dark eyes sparkling. 'You may as well come into the water yourself now that you are wet,' she said in her clear if somewhat stilted English. 'It is more than an hour since we ate luncheon.'

Time she stirred herself to some form of activity, Zoe conceded. Getting to her feet, she scooped the length of her hair back into her nape with a slide before stepping lithely forward to dive into the water. Blue tiles slid past her eyes as she made for the far end of the pool. She surfaced exhilarated and with breath to spare in the shallow end, to find her erstwhile teaser almost up with her.

'You were right,' she declared. 'This is far better than lazing!'

'Until it is time to dress and drive to the Plaka?' came the reminder. 'You had not forgotten?'

Zoe shook her head. 'I hadn't forgotten. There isn't much point in getting there before five-thirty when the shops open for business again, though, is there?'

'But we are to eat dinner there?'

'Whatever *you'd* like to do.'

'I have visited the Plaka district only rarely before you came,' stated the Greek girl, 'and never in the evening. Alexis says it is still rather too orientated towards the tourists.'

'From what I've seen of it on previous visits to Athens, I'd say he had a point,' Zoe agreed, 'but I still think it's one of the most appealing places to wander around in for a few hours. After all, it is the oldest part of Athens and one can see there how the city looked one hundred years ago. I thought we might eat at a taverna. There's one I remember in particular from last time I was there, if I can find it again. Sidrivani, I think it was called.'

The other laughed. 'We will find it if we have to search the whole quarter!'

'You're quite sure your brother will approve of our going there in the evening?' asked Zoe, and saw a faint cloud cross the lovely young features for a moment.

'Why should he not approve when it was he himself who wished for me to have an English companion who would show me the ways of your countryfolk?'

'But it was your sister who actually appointed me.'

'Only because Christa lives in England and could conduct interviews more easily than he could himself, as she told us when she brought you here. He would naturally trust her to make the right choice.'

He must have done, Zoe reflected. In which case, why should she have this feeling of trepidation at the thought of Alexis Theodorou's homecoming tomorrow? She and Sofia had done nothing during the week she had been here at the Villa Mimosa that anyone might find fault with.

One week. Was that really all it was? Since the very first day she had felt so much at home, despite the unaccustomed luxury of being waited on hand and foot. Being Greek, the staff didn't consider themselves in any way servile by doing the job for which they were paid. Her efforts to improve her grasp of their language had been greeted with humour and delight by one and all.

Sofia herself was a darling. A great deal less gregarious than her equivalent in Britain, of course, but only because of her circumstances. At eighteen she knew little of the world outside her own country apart from what she had learned out of books. The furthest she had ever travelled was to the outlying islands on the family yacht.

Her brother must shoulder the lion's share of blame for that lack—a subscriber to the old school of thought concerning the female sex in general, it appeared. That in hiring a foreign companion for his young sister he showed signs of a change in attitude was all to the good, if somewhat puzzling. It seemed odd that a man such as Alexis Theodorou was reputed to be should see the need for change at all, much less leave a woman who had shown little regard for family custom in marrying a foreigner herself to choose said companion—*and* another foreigner at that.

Meeting Christa Townsend for the first time at her initial interview, Zoe had been struck by the woman's unclouded beauty. Judging from the fact that she had acknowledged having lived in England for nineteen years since her marriage, Christa had to be in her mid to late thirties, yet she could pass for twenty-eight, twenty-nine at the most. Happiness had to be a contributory factor.

Her young sister, Sofia, had been born the year after her own departure from the family fold—by way of a replacement, she had said in an honest and open summary of the more immediate Theodorou history. That birth had cost the mother her life, for which loss both the first- and last-born daughters of the house had carried the burden of blame. In Christa's case this had meant a total severance of all communication, in Sofia's an upbringing in strict Greek tradition to ensure that she, at least, had little or no contact at all with foreigners of any nationality.

Nicolas Theodorou's death from a heart attack ten years ago had left his only son, Alexis, in charge of both the family business affairs, and Sofia herself at an age when most young men were still in the process of finding their feet in the world at large. He had gone against his father's wishes both in renewing the bond with his older sister, and in allowing Sofia to attend schools where English was regarded as a second and essential tongue, but that had been the limit of his deviation, it seemed to Zoe, until this request for an English companion to be found now that Sofia had completed her schooling. A radical change indeed, from every angle.

Not that Mrs Townsend had been anything but diligent in her approach to the matter. Zoe's background had been thoroughly probed, her educational qualifications checked out. Considering the number of applicants, it had been a considerable boost to be offered the post. She was here now for a year, and it already showed promise of being a good one.

'Zoe?' The questioning tone brought her out of her reverie with a start. She smiled at the younger girl, who was watching her with curious eyes.

'Sorry, I was miles away! What would you like to do?'

'I would like you to teach me how to swim the butterfly stroke you do so well,' came the diffident reply. 'But only if you feel like doing so, of course.'

'I'd enjoy it,' Zoe replied truthfully, resolving to eradicate that diffidence if it was the last thing she did. Sofia asked so little of life—probably because she had experienced so comparatively little of it up to now.

Teaching her to swim butterfly-style was a minor thing, but it was a tribute to their emerging relationship that the girl had made the request at all. A week ago she would have been content to wait until Zoe herself made a suggestion.

They spent the following twenty minutes or so on the lesson. A fair swimmer, but lacking the strength of muscle, Sofia found the stroke difficult to master.

'It will come,' Zoe promised. 'We can practise every day.' She added lightly, 'In the meantime, I still owe you for that splashing, don't I?'

Face alight with laughter, Sofia threw up her hands to ward off the spray of water Zoe sent surging over her, then promptly retaliated. The battle which followed was both noisy and messy, soaking the paved surround in the vicinity as the splashes grew wilder.

The realisation of another presence struck Zoe first, causing her to miss her footing as she made to turn and look, and go under. Surfacing again bare seconds later, she saw Sofia gazing at the man standing at the pool-edge, her face reflecting oddly conflicting emotions.

'You were not expected home until tomorrow, Alexis,' she said in English.

One black brow lifted, lending the strongly carved features a certain sardonicism. He answered in the same language, the depth and timbre of his voice underlining his fundamental musculinity.

'So I arrive a day early. Will you not introduce me to your companion?'

'I'm Zoe Searston, *kyrie*,' supplied the latter, suppressing her discomfiture at the manner of their meeting. 'I apologise for all the noise.'

'You weren't the only one producing it,' he returned. His English was heavily accented but far less structured than Sofia's, Zoe noted. 'I wasn't aware that my sister was acquainted with any English people.'

Zoe looked back at him in some confusion. 'I'm the one you asked Kyria Townsend to find, *kyrie*. A companion for Sofia.'

If there had been any humour at all in the dark eyes it certainly wasn't there now. He looked positively thunderstruck. 'I asked for no such thing!' he declared. 'What kind of a game is this?'

Stunned beyond speech by the caustic denial, Zoe could only gaze at him in bewilderment. Beside her, Sofia remained unmoving too, both of them frozen like pillars of salt—except that salt would have dissolved by now, came the irrelevant thought.

'I . . . don't understand,' she got out. 'Kyria Townsend said she was acting for you in making the appointment.'

The firmly cut mouth took on a thinner line. 'Had I considered such a step, I would have entrusted the task to no one but myself. Neither,' he added, 'would there have been any question of looking beyond my own countrywomen.' He shifted his attention abruptly to his sister, eyes narrowing as he surveyed the lovely face. 'Did you know anything of this?'

Her hesitation was fleeting, but long enough to suggest a degree of evasion in the answer. 'I only know what Christa told me.'

'I don't believe you,' came the flat statement. 'You will both of you come out of there and put on some clothing, and then we'll get to the truth.'

Sofia was first to make a move to obey the injunction. She cast an apologetic glance in Zoe's direction before heading for the steps. Zoe followed more slowly, aware of her clinging suit and thankful that she was at least wearing a reasonably modest one-piece.

Dark eyes openly appraised her as she hoisted herself from the water in Sofia's wake and moved at her side towards him, starting at her feet and taking in every detail of her slender curves on the way to her face, framed within sleeked and water-darkened hair. She felt her colour coming up, the bite of her nails as her fingers curled involuntarily into the palms of her hands.

Around five feet ten or so in height himself, he had the build of a gymnast, with broad shoulders tapering down to a narrow waist and hipline. His legs in the dark grey trousers looked strong and muscular, the overall impression one of power under firm control. An Alpha man in every respect, came the fleeting thought, eliciting a sudden and unwonted aversion.

'I'm not sure what all this is about,' she said forcefully when she reached him, 'but I object to your attitude, *kyrie*! If there is a fault, it's neither mine nor Sofia's.'

'That,' he said without raising his voice, 'is what we are about to discuss. But only when you're both of you more suitably clad. You have wraps?'

'On the loungers over there,' Zoe acknowledged.

'Then go and put them on.' He indicated the table and chairs set out near by. 'I'll wait here.'

Walking away under that same scrutiny was even more unnerving than walking towards him. Zoe could feel the tension in her spine, the stiffness in her legs as she moved.

'*Do* you know more than you're letting on, Sofia?' she asked quietly when she calculated that they were out of earshot.

'It was Christa's idea for me to have an English companion,' came the bleak confession. 'She believed that if Alexis returned from his business trip to find the arrangement already in force he would accept it more readily than if she asked his opinion first. I wanted to believe it too, so I closed my mind to any doubts. I have so enjoyed your company, Zoe, as I knew that I would the moment that we met. It will be so hard now to lose you.'

'I haven't gone yet,' returned Zoe with suddenly renewed spirit. 'Nor do I intend to—at least not without
a fight!'

'If Alexis says that you must, then you must. He will
allow no argument.'

'From you, perhaps not, but I have a contract for the
year.'

'Arranged with my sister, not Alexis. He will not consider it binding.'

'We'll see.'

Zoe spoke with more certainty than she felt, but there
was no point in giving up before she had even heard
what Alexis Theodorou had to say. She had taken a
sabbatical from her teaching career for this job. Should
she have to return to England, there was no guarantee
that she would be able to walk straight into another position. That the same would apply next year was beside
the point. That was then, this was now.

Clad in the white towelling robe, she felt scarcely less
vulnerable. Those eyes of his could pierce steel! He remained standing after seeing the two of them seated in
the comfortably padded chairs, leaning his weight against
the table to look from one to the other in unsmiling
regard. Cut short to fit the shape of his head like a ram's
tightly curled fleece, the thick black hair was repeated
in the apex of his open-necked white shirt. Tie and jacket
removed on arrival home, surmised Zoe.

'So?' he said.

She took care to iron out any hint of defensiveness
from her voice. 'It's all quite straightforward. I responded to an advertisement placed by Kyria Townsend,
was interviewed on three separate occasions and finally
granted the position for one year.'

'On a salary paid by whom?'

'I didn't ask. An account was opened here at an Athens
bank for me with my first month's payment in advance.

I imagine Kyria Townsend arranged it herself when she brought me here.' Zoe paused to draw a steadying breath, aware of the unrelenting hardness of his mouth. 'So far as I knew, she was acting on your behalf, *kyrie*. Why should I think otherwise?'

'Why indeed?' It was Sofia's turn to undergo the penetrating scrutiny. 'You said you know only what Christa told you. Am I to understand that you had no prior awareness of the arrangement at all?'

Sofia bent her head. 'We are both at fault.'

She had spoken in Greek; her brother said sharply, 'We will use English.'

'I speak a little Greek,' Zoe interjected, and immediately felt a complete idiot as he gave her a scathing glance.

'A little is scarcely enough. Not that there appears to be so very much more to be said on the subject at present.' He straightened away from the table with a jerky movement redolent of held-in anger. 'I go now to telephone my sister. You, *despinis*, will come to the study in half an hour, fully dressed.'

Sofia looked up again, eyes anxious. 'You are going to send Zoe away?'

'That,' he said, 'is not a matter for discussion.'

'But I do not want her to go.' There was a pleading note in her voice. 'Zoe is my friend, Alexis. The very best friend I ever had! You cannot know how much I have enjoyed her company while you have been away.'

'You have other friends,' he said. 'Of your own kind.'

'Of the same class, you mean?' put in Zoe with taut intonation. 'For your information, *kyrie*, I'm not exactly out of the gutter myself. Kyria Townsend went very thoroughly into my background.'

'I'm quite sure of it,' came the unmoved response. 'I was referring to nationality. You can have little concept of our way of life.'

'When it comes to keeping girls under lock and key, you're right!' She was leaning forward in her chair, eyes sparking like emeralds, temperance abandoned. 'Did you never hear of emancipation?'

The black brows rose again. '*Lock* and *key*?'

Zoe flushed a little. 'Well, all right, so that was perhaps going a bit far. All the same, compared with English girls Sofia's age——'

'Considering some of the English girls Sofia's age that I've met with myself, I'd say that a little of the same protective discipline wouldn't go amiss,' Alexis cut in drily. 'You'd have me allow my sister to wander the streets half-dressed, the way your countrywomen do?' He shook his head as she opened her mouth to reply. 'Enough of this. I'll see you in half an hour.'

Zoe watched in helpless fury as he strode up the flight of stone steps leading to the terrace of the big white-walled villa that was the Theodorou home from home. The man's sheer arrogance set her teeth on edge. That his intention was to send her packing there was little doubt. His sister's pleas meant nothing to him.

'How can he be like that?' she burst out. 'What right does any man have to be so...uncaring?'

'Alexis is my guardian as well as my brother,' said Sofia. 'And he does care for me very much. He is angry now because of Christa's actions, but he is not always so stern. He would give me anything I desired.'

'Except the freedom to pick and choose your friends, it seems. Or to go anywhere on your own, for that matter.'

The other sighed. 'It is not always safe for a girl on her own. I understand that. And I do choose my own friends. It is just that...'

'Just that they have to be from a certain sphere,' supplied Zoe when Sofia failed to complete the sentence. 'I can appreciate the concern, but not the restriction.'

'There is no forcible restriction,' Sofia protested. 'Should I wish to, I could go wherever I liked.'

'With dire penalties to be paid, I imagine.'

'Not that either. Alexis would not dream of inflicting chastisement.' She spread her hands. 'It is not the way you think, Zoe. I obey because I see the good sense in what Alexis says is right for me.'

It was Zoe's turn to sigh. 'You're right, of course. I'm the one in the wrong for attempting to undermine the whole structure. Not that it's going to make a great deal of difference. I have a feeling I shan't even be seeing out the day.'

'I shall miss you so much,' said the younger girl wryly. 'I have learned a great deal from you.'

'While I, it seems, have learned very little.' Zoe got to her feet. 'I'd better go and dress if I'm to be on time for my appointment. I'd hate to keep your brother waiting.'

Sofia sighed. 'He is not accustomed to being so.'

Zoe could imagine. When Alexis Theodorou said jump he would expect, and no doubt get, instant compliance. There was no point in trying to prove herself the exception. To even attempt it by being a few minutes late would only serve to underline a certain lack of maturity on her part, and that was the last thing she wanted to suggest to this male autocrat.

Sofia made no attempt to accompany her indoors. Zoe left her slumped in the chair, looking thoroughly unhappy.

As villas went, Mimosa had to be in a class of its own, Zoe thought, not for the first time, as she approached the building. Set within gardens massed in flowers and scattered with marble statues, its sparkling white stonework was embellished with neoclassical Doric columns, iron balustrades and pediments above the many windows. Although little more than half an hour's

journey from central Athens with its teeming traffic,
here, in the beautiful suburb of Politia, in the foothills
of Penteli the air was fresh and clean, the pace un-
hurried. The best of both worlds, Zoe had judged on
arrival, and had seen no reason to alter that opinion
since.

Inside, the villa had been stripped of pretension and
refurbished with typical Greek understatement. No car-
peting on the ground floor, the pale gold polished wood
setting off to perfection the gilt of Italian mirrors, the
glowing colours of the artwork and fine rugs. The furnishings were a clever and comfortable mixture of the
old and the new, the whole redolent of wealth allied to
superb good taste. Alexis's own choice, Sofia had said,
and one with which Zoe could find no fault.

The bedroom allocated to her was furnished in light
wood and decorated in pastel shades. Blue as the sea,
and almost as deep, the carpet sprang thick and soft beneath her feet. There was an adjoining superbly fitted
bathroom, and a dressing area with enough wardrobe
space for half a dozen people, much less one.

At the very least it wasn't going to take her long to
pack, she thought wryly, towelling her hair after a shower
and trying to decide what she should wear. Not that it
really mattered what kind of impression she made on
Alexis Theodorou now.

His sister's actions took some understanding. While
able to appreciate that Christa might have felt moved to
open up her young sister's life a little, how could she
possibly have thought to get away with her ruse once
Alexis returned home? Right now he was no doubt on
the telephone telling her exactly what *he* thought of her
machinations; Zoe could well imagine the cutting tones.
It was doubtful if Christa would be able to convince him
to allow her to stay. His whole attitude was adamantly
against the idea.

The mirrored walls reflected her image from all sides—
a novelty which had in itself taken a little getting used
to. Her skin was beginning to acquire a light tan already,
she noted, making her eyes look a deeper green and
lending her face a healthy, sun-kissed glow. Springing
back into its natural curl as it dried, her hair fell in a
copper cloud about her bare shoulders. She seized a
brush and tried to smooth it down into some semblance
of order, briefly contemplated tying it back into her nape
again, then shrugged and left it lying loose. Why bother?

Wearing a straight-cut cream skirt and green striped
blouse, she made her way downstairs again. The study
was off the rear of the hall, she knew, although she had
not so far had reason to enter the room. She waited now
for the minute hand of her watch to reach the exact time
before knocking on the heavy door. The command to
enter was terse and discouraging—had she needed any
further discouragement. She mentally girded her loins
as she went on in.

Alexis Theodorou was seated at a desk with his back
to the window. A modern, well-equipped office containing little in the way of home comforts, was Zoe's
initial impression of the room. She took the chair he
indicated, and waited resignedly for the axe to fall. From
the expression on the olive-skinned features, it was certainly coming.

'I've spoken with my sister,' he said. 'She'll be arriving here tomorrow afternoon to return you to
England.'

Zoe's chin lifted. 'I don't need a chaperon, *kyrie*. I'm
more than capable of seeing myself home.'

'That I've no doubt,' he returned. 'But you will, all
the same, be accompanied. You'll receive a further two
months' salary in lieu of notice.'

She looked back at him steadily. 'Kyrie Theodorou,
you can obviously dismiss me from my employment, but

you can't force me to leave the country until I'm good and ready.'

His shrug spoke volumes. 'Why would you wish to stay? In the hope that I might change my mind?'

Zoe cast caution to the winds. 'I doubt if you ever do that, *kyrie*, even where you're proved wrong. To acknowledge error is to show weakness, and no Greek male would countenance such loss of face!'

The dark eyes took on a glint almost of amusement. 'You speak with more bravado than sense. What would an English woman know of *perifania*?'

'Oh, we have self-esteem too,' she countered. 'Only we don't take it to the same extremes. Kyria Townsend flouted your authority; therefore we all of us have to pay the price. Perhaps if you asked yourself just why she felt the need to go behind your back in this instance you might come up with a reasonable answer.'

Her omission of the formal address did not go unnoted. He studied her in silence for a moment, brows drawn together. When he did speak again it was abruptly. 'How old are you?'

Zoe frowned herself, but saw no good reason to refuse an answer. 'I'm twenty-three.'

'Old enough to have learned something of diplomacy. We're not here to discuss my sister's motives. She and I will do that alone.'

'It doesn't take much working out,' Zoe responded, refusing to be put down. 'She considers Sofia to be deprived of contact outside her own narrow little world. At eighteen she should be stepping out, experiencing new places, meeting new people. I'm sure you did all of that.'

'A different matter.'

'It shouldn't be. Not in this day and age.' She made some attempt to find a better basis for understanding. 'I appreciate the protective instinct inherent in the Greek where their womenfolk are concerned, *kyrie*, only it can become overpowering. Sofia has everything anyone could ever want in the material sense, but there's more to life than that.'

His lips thinned. 'You take a great many liberties.'

'I don't have anything to lose,' she pointed out undauntedly. 'Sofia does. We'd intended visiting the Plaka together this evening. Just to browse through the shops and explore, and perhaps eat at a taverna. She was looking forward to it so much. As I'm obviously not going to have the opportunity now to go with her, perhaps you'd care to take her yourself so as not to disappoint her.'

'I have more to do than visit the Plaka!'

'As I'm sure you always have. In your position, you can have no shortage of underlings well able to run things if you wanted a break from business commitments, so it has to be choice.'

'The fact that I don't care to browse through the Plaka district doesn't mean that Sofia and I spend no time together,' he returned shortly.

'But you're away quite a lot, which necessarily limits the time you *can* spend together.' Zoe paused, assessing his expression and wondering if she dared make a further suggestion. May as well be hanged for a sheep as for a lamb, she supposed. 'If Kyria Townsend is coming over, why not consider letting her take Sofia back to London with her for a holiday? After all, she's *her* sister, too.'

One palm came down hard on the surface of the desk, making everything on it rattle. 'Enough of this. You go too far!'

Stubborn to the last, Zoe stood—or sat—her ground. 'It was just an idea. I didn't really think you'd agree to it.'

'Then it was waste of time in even mentioning it.' He looked at her in exasperation. 'Are you deliberately trying to anger me?'

She looked back at him without flinching. 'I've grown very fond of Sofia. I think she merits any effort I can make to get through to you. If you won't allow me to befriend her, then you can at least make sure she has someone else she likes and trusts well enough to turn to when you're not available. And I don't mean one of the so-called friends I've met during the past week. They're mostly only drawn by the fact that she's a Theodorou.'

'You don't,' he said, 'give her much credit as an individual.'

'I give her every credit,' Zoe came back with force. 'She has the sweetest nature of anyone I ever met! I suppose, if the truth were known, you have a husband already selected for her with a family name to equal your own. Orestes Antoniou, for instance? He called on her the other day.'

Alexis studied her with unreadable expression. 'I gather you didn't approve of him?'

'I found him objectionably condescending,' Zoe confessed. 'Not just to me, but to Sofia too. He acted as if he already owned the place!'

'Is that so?' The tone was non-committal. 'Once again——'

'I know. It isn't a matter for discussion.' She added levelly, 'I can only hope that Sofia will refuse to marry *any* man she doesn't love!'

The strong mouth twisted. 'Love isn't essential to a good marriage. There are other factors far more important.'

'To you, perhaps, but Sofia needs to love and be loved. She detests Orestes!'

'She told you this?'

'She didn't need to say it.'

'Ah, I see, you're a reader of minds!'

Zoe hesitated. She hadn't meant to go this far; the words kept forming themselves. On the other hand, why not? He couldn't fire her twice.

'In Sofia's case, yes. We have an affinity despite the five years between us. You'll ruin her whole life if you force her into a marriage she doesn't want with a man she has no feeling for.'

'There's no question of force.'

'There is if she believes it's what *you* want. In any case,' she added, 'she's far too young to be marrying anyone.'

Alexis was silent for a lengthy moment, his regard penetrating. Zoe felt the thudding of her heart against her ribcage, as if she had been running hard, a sense of wonder at her own temerity. Until now she had never considered herself particularly outspoken. But then she had never felt quite so deeply about anything as she did about this.

'Tell me something about yourself,' he invited unexpectedly.

Disconcerted, she took a moment to gather her thoughts. 'Didn't Kyria Townsend already do that?'

'I was in no mood to listen,' he acknowledged with a glimmer of dry humour. 'And better direct from—how do you say it—the horse's lips?' The smile was little more than a twitch of his own lips. 'Not that you in any way resemble that animal.'

He could probably, Zoe reflected fleetingly, be quite the charmer when he put his mind to it. His request was confusing. Why should he have any interest in her background if he intended getting rid of her? Unless there was a chance that he might be changing his mind on that score? She could only go along with him, and hope.

'My home is in the Midlands,' she said, 'although I live and work in the south of England. Did, up until a couple of weeks ago, that is. My father is a lecturer in

English literature at a local university; my mother doesn't have a job as such, but she's very much involved in charity work for various organisations. I teach geography at preparatory-school level.'

'For how long?'

'Eighteen months or so.'

There was no telling anything now from Alexis Theodorou's expression. 'You were unhappy in your work?'

'No,' she acknowledged, sensing what was coming. 'It just didn't fulfil me the way I thought it would. I chose geography as my main subject chiefly because I've always had this interest in other countries. Seeing this job advertised seemed like manna from heaven at the time. I've been to Greece several times before—although only on holiday—and I couldn't resist the idea of spending a whole year here.'

'Even though it meant giving up your career as a teacher?'

'Interrupting,' she amended. 'I can always start over again.'

'You may not find it such an easy thing to get another post.'

Too true, she thought wryly. Aloud she said, 'I shall have to meet that problem if and when I come to it.'

'You can scarcely do it before. What were your parents' reactions when you told them you were giving up teaching in order to take this post?'

'Predictable,' she admitted. 'The fact that I would be working for the Theodorou family was one of the few points in favour. My father did some research into *your* background, *kyrie*. Your name is known and respected both here and abroad.'

He acknowledged the comment with a sardonic tilt of his head. 'You're too kind.'

Too close to obsequiousness, Zoe regretted. He didn't need telling such things; he already knew his position.

'If that's all,' she said evenly, getting up, 'I'll go and start packing my things.'

For a brief moment he looked almost startled—unaccustomed, she gathered, to having an interview terminated by anyone but himself. Well, tough! If she was leaving anyway, there was little need for further kowtowing.

'You'll have plenty of time for that,' he declared. 'My sister won't be here before tomorrow afternoon, and will certainly be staying overnight.'

'Am I to be allowed any contact with Sofia in the meantime?' she asked, and saw his mouth take on a slant.

'Short of confining the two of you to your rooms, I see no way of keeping you apart. But you'll stay here at Mimosa. I'll inform Yannis that his services are no longer needed.'

'I was proposing to drive myself,' Zoe admitted. 'I hold a licence, and I have experience of driving on the right-hand side.'

'In Athens itself?'

'On occasion, yes.'

He studied her with interest. 'You don't find the traffic intimidating?'

'No more so than in central London.' She tagged on levelly, 'If I didn't have confidence in myself as a driver, I wouldn't be on the road at all. I'm certainly not intimidated by aggressive male horn-pushers. We have those in England too.'

'I'm fast reaching the conclusion,' came the ironic reply, 'that very little frightens you. You might do well to remember that one can be *too* confident.' He inclined his head. 'You may go now.'

Trust him to have the last word, she thought wrath-fully as she turned to leave the room. She had the feeling that Alexis Theodorou would make sure he always did.

CHAPTER TWO

SOFIA came out from the nearby *saloni* as Zoe emerged from the study. Dressed now in full-skirted white cotton, her dark hair cascading about her shoulders, the younger girl looked like a princess.

'You were a long time with Alexis,' she said. 'I have been waiting here for many minutes to hear what he had to say.'

'Nothing encouraging,' Zoe acknowledged. 'Your sister is coming tomorrow in order to take me back to England. Not that I've any intention of missing the Easter holiday now that I'm here. I'll book into a hotel for the next couple of weeks.'

'It may not be easy to find a room at such a time,' warned Sofia. 'It is a very busy period.'

'I can only try.' Zoe lightened her voice. 'I'm afraid the Plaka visit is out, but we still have a couple of days together. Let's make the most of them.'

By tacit consent, the coming severance wasn't mentioned again during the rest of the afternoon and early evening. As in most Greek households, dinner was served late. Seated on either side of the long table, with Alexis at its head, the two girls had little inclination to chat during the meal the way they had become accustomed to doing. It was left to Alexis himself to make what conversation there was, which he did without apparently noticing the monosyllabic replies.

Wearing casual trousers and a shirt in a deep cream colour, he looked devastatingly attractive, Zoe was bound to admit. Why, in his mid-thirties, he still re-

mained unmarried, she couldn't begin to imagine. If for
no other reason than securing the future of the
Theodorou lineage, he should surely be thinking about
taking a wife and starting a family? Finding a woman
of the right kind to fill such a role wouldn't be difficult;
he could no doubt have his pick from a whole host of
eligible females. Love, as he had said earlier, was the
least requirement.

Served warm rather than piping hot, as was common
in Greece, the skewered squares of swordfish grilled with
tomatoes and onion, which constituted the main course
of the meal, were still delicious, but for once Zoe found
herself unable to do justice to cooking that was well
above average.

'Is the *xifia* not to your liking?' asked Alexis mildly,
watching her toy with the dish. 'Perhaps you might prefer
something else?'

'No, no, this is fine!' she assured him. 'I'm just not
very hungry, that's all.'

'You ate little of the *dolmathes*, either,' he observed.
'Are you not feeling well?'

She looked at him then, a long, steady look which
elicited a sudden spark in the dark eyes. 'Losing one's
job is hardly scheduled to increase the appetite, *kyrie*.'

'True,' he agreed. 'Just as arriving home to find one's
authority usurped is unlikely to improve the temper.' He
paused, expression unrevealing. 'I realise now that you
yourself acted in good faith, and can't be blamed for
any of this.'

Zoe stared at him, aware that Sofia too had caught
the inflexion in his voice and was also gazing at him in
newly awakened hope. 'Are you saying you might be
having second thoughts about getting rid of me?' she
asked tentatively.

The smile was faint. 'Shall we say that I've decided
to give you a trial period in which to prove yourself.'

'Alexis!' Sofia was overjoyed and making no effort to conceal it. 'Thank you! You cannot know what this means to me!'

'It means only that Miss Searston stays for now,' he returned, 'not that your whole life is about to change overnight.' His glance came back to Zoe, who was still trying to take in this volte-face. 'I shall want your assurance that you go nowhere and do nothing that I don't first approve.'

She shook herself to reply. 'Of course. That goes without saying.'

'It does?' He tilted an ironic lip. 'I hadn't imagined unquestioning obedience to be one of your qualities.'

Zoe kept her own expression carefully bland. 'If you can make concessions, *kyrie*, so can I.'

'You will call me Alexis,' he said, surprising her yet again. 'Too much formality could become irksome.'

Who said a leopard couldn't change its spots? she thought confusedly. This was a different man from the one she had met for the first time so few hours before. Relaxed from that inflexible line, his mouth held a certain sensuality, sending a faint tremor along her spine. A man different from *any* she had ever met with before, if it came to that.

'What about Kyria Townsend?' she asked.

'I already telephoned her again and told her she no longer needed to make the journey.'

'Christa must have been surprised,' said Sofia.

Broad shoulders lifted. 'More delighted that her stratagem succeeded after all.' To Zoe, he added, 'She appears to regard you very highly.'

'If she hadn't,' returned the latter, 'I don't suppose she would have considered bringing me here in the first place. She has Sofia's welfare as much at heart as you do yourself.'

'I have never been so happy as I am at this moment!' declared the younger girl, drawing a suddenly wry glance from her brother. 'Now that I have a true friend and companion, I shall not mind so much when you have to go away again.'

'It will be some time before I have need to,' he said. 'After the Easter festivities, I intend to take the yacht down through the islands and visit our relatives. You'd like that?'

'Oh, yes!' Her face was lit. 'It is so long since I last saw them all. Zoe could come too, of course?'

'Of course.' Black eyes met green, expression difficult to define. 'You like the sea?'

'Very much,' Zoe returned truthfully. 'Though I'm not experienced in the crewing department.'

'The *Hestia* is driven by engine power, not sail, and carries a crew of eight,' Alexis responded matter-of-factly.

'Is it to be just the three of us?' asked Sofia, her smile fading just a little as he shook his head.

'There will be others too, of course. We'll only be using three of the cabins ourselves.'

Exactly how large *was* this yacht? wondered Zoe. A cruise through the islands sounded good, although she too would have preferred a more casual affair. As Sofia's paid companion, she was hardly going to be on level pegging with the invited guests.

Another bridge she would cross if and when she came to it, she told herself firmly. For the present, it mattered only that she would be going at all.

The sweet *tyropita* served as dessert went down like a dream. Made from feta cheese mashed with milk and eggs and baked into a pie, it was one of Zoe's favourites. Tiny cups of the thick and heavy coffee which she had learned never to refer to as Turkish completed the meal.

Both Alexis and Sofia took it laden with sugar to a degree that made her shudder inwardly. It must, she thought, be like drinking syrup! It had taken her several days to convince the staff that she actually preferred the stuff *sketo*—without sugar—herself. The like-minded housekeeper, Artemis, who had been with the family since Nicolas Theodorou himself was a boy, had proclaimed her in need of some extra flesh on her bones to make her more attractive to real men, who preferred a woman more rounded, and had not yet given up hope of adding those extra pounds.

To the Greek mind, a meal was something to be lingered over. At least when at home, Alexis proved himself no exception to the rule by showing little inclination to terminate the occasion. Once the evening temperatures had reached a suitable level, Sofia had said, dinner would be served outside on the terrace, as was luncheon now. Zoe looked forward to that. Eating under the stars was a treat for anyone born and bred in a climate which all too rarely allowed such freedom.

It was gone eleven o'clock when they finally left the table. Alexis took himself off on business unspecified after saying goodnight, leaving Zoe feeling just a little flat. Reaction from the events of the afternoon, she told herself. It had been shock on shock.

His change of mind still puzzled her. It seemed so totally out of character for the man. Yet how could she say that for certain when she didn't even know him? Out of character for the man she had judged him to be was more like it. It just went to show that first impressions were not always so reliable.

In bed before midnight, she felt too restless for sleep. A trial period only was all she had been promised. One step out of line, and Alexis could still rescind on the decision. He had made a big concession in allowing her to stay on at all; she didn't want him to regret it. All the same, she had no intention of playing the total subservient either.

Eventually, still wide awake, she got up again and pulled on a pair of trousers and a lightweight sweater. The grounds were extensive enough for quite a lengthy stroll. Better to be out in the fresh air and doing something than lying here waiting for sleep that wouldn't come. The moon was almost full, the light more than adequate. Half an hour or so should do the trick.

She left the villa via one of the rooms opening on to the wide, stone-flagged terrace. Scent from the profusion of plant life spilling from tall stone urns filled the air, overlaid with the more subtle hint of eucalyptus. It was cool by comparison with the day, but far from chilly. Zoe felt she could stay out all night.

Skirting the pool, she made her way along a path that wound between banks of hibiscus bushes. At the far end lay a little circular temple built of white stone, its roof supported by statues of the ancient Greek goddesses. Stone seating ran around the inside perimeter. Her footsteps faltered as her eyes fell on the human figure at rest there.

Alexis had already heard her approach and was looking in her direction, so there was no point in attempting to fade back into the bushes. She went forward slowly as he came to his feet.

'I'm sorry,' she said. 'I didn't mean to disturb you. I couldn't sleep, and thought a walk might help.'

'No matter,' he returned. 'I was taking the air myself before retiring. We'll walk together.'

It was the last thing she had expected him to say, and the last thing she wanted right now. Alexis Theodorou disturbed her in a way she found difficult to deal with. His very masculinity tautened her stomach muscles, arousing a deep-down ache to which she didn't want to put a name. To be out here in the moonlit darkness with him was far from sleep-inducing; she had never felt more wide awake.

Moving at her side along the gravelled paths which meandered through the informal gardens, he maintained an initial silence. In her flat-heeled shoes, she came no higher than his jawline. His breadth of shoulder made her feel almost fragile by comparison.

The orange glow that was central Athens filled the sky to the south, hiding the stars. Down in the islands, the skies would be clear of traffic pollution, the stars sparkling like diamonds against thick black velvet. She had always wanted to cruise the Cyclades—so named because they supposedly circled the sacred island of Delos, birthplace of Apollo. In early May, when they would travel, the tourist season would not yet be into its stride.

'I must thank you again for allowing me to stay on,' she said at length. 'Would it be presumptuous of me to ask what it was that changed your mind?'

His shrug was brief, his tone unrevealing. 'Perhaps the realisation that Sofia is no longer a child, and has desires of her own. It hasn't been easy these last years, carrying out my father's wishes.'

Zoe cast a swift glance at the hard-edged profile. 'Would he approve of my being here?'

'No, he wouldn't.' It was a bare statement of fact. 'He had no love of the English.'

'Because of losing his daughter to an Englishman?'

'The hostility went back much further than that. He was once left to bear the brunt of a fraudulent deal effected by an English company. He swore on oath never to trust your people again.'

'You can't condemn a whole race for the actions of a few,' Zoe protested. 'That's bigotry!'

'Call it what you will. That was how he felt.'

'And you? Do you distrust the English in business too?'

'No more than any other nationality—including my own. In business one places one's entire trust in no one.'

'That's a very cynical viewpoint. By the law of averages, there have to be some honest people around.' She added purposefully, 'Yourself, for instance. You're surely not admitting to shady practices under the Theodorou name?'

'None that I'm aware of, but that doesn't mean it never happens. As you yourself pointed out, I have underlings capable of running things in my stead. How can one ever be sure that all is above board?'

'You'd know,' Zoe stated with certainty. 'You'd always keep your finger on the pulse!'

His laugh was low, tremoring a response in the pit of her stomach. 'You're very quick to judge—perhaps too quick. You know little of me.'

'I know of your reputation,' she said. 'If there was anything shady about your business affairs, my father would have picked up on it. As one of Europe's top industrialists at such a comparatively early age, you have a lot to be proud of.' She left the subject abruptly, aware of coming close once again to sycophancy. She would hate for him to think her a boot-licker. 'Was it just to follow your father's wishes that you kept Sofia from following a more independent lifestyle, or is it your own opinion that women should be dominated by the male as a matter of course?'

He gave her an oblique glance, brows quizzically lifted. 'I take it you object to such an idea yourself?'

'All the way.' She was in no doubt on that score. 'Given the opportunity, women are just as capable as men of looking after their own interests. I can see that the old ways might still hold sway in the countryside, where tourism hasn't encroached too much yet—but in the towns, particularly Athens, things have surely changed? Girls take jobs outside the home. They live their own lives the way they want to.'

'On the surface, perhaps.' Alexis sounded tolerantly amused. 'Make no mistake about it, the majority of our women still know their place, and accord the menfolk of their family the respect they're due. It's a brother's duty to safeguard his sister's virtue against all who may offer her temptation. Many men would not consider taking a wife who had already given herself to another.'

'That's an antediluvian attitude,' Zoe declared. 'I'd be willing to bet the same rule doesn't apply to men!'

'A different matter,' came the anticipated reply. 'A man has needs.'

'So, believe it or not, do women. Why should they be bound by rules no man would accept?'

There was a lengthy pause before he said softly, 'Do I assume that you yourself are bound by no such rules?'

Zoe drew in a breath. She had left herself wide open to that interpretation, but he still had no right to put such a question.

'My personal life is my own affair,' she said stiffly.

'Not in this instance.' He had come to a halt, blocking her further passage. His eyes were like black coals. 'If you wish to retain your position here, you'll answer the question.'

Zoe gazed at him uncertainly, conscious of having talked herself into a cleft stick. The very idea of baring her innermost self to anyone was unpalatable, although to refuse outright after what he had just said would put him in a position where keeping his word would be his only way of saving face. Compromise was the only possible alternative.

'I won't answer the question the way it was put because I don't think you have any right to ask it,' she said with control. 'All I'm disputing is the *assumption* that a woman should remain a virgin until she marries, while a man has freedom to indulge his appetites where and when he fancies without any form of censure.'

'Just a great deal of risk in this day and age if he follows that creed,' came the dry reply. 'No man of any sense at all would indulge himself imprudently.' He studied her face, his expression veiled by shadow. 'You're very stubborn.'

'Only when I'm pressured,' she returned. 'I may work for you, *kyrie*, but you don't own me body and soul.'

'So it appears.' He paused, added softly, 'You were to call me by name. Do you find Alexis so difficult to say?'

'Difficult to adopt,' Zoe admitted. 'I'm an employee, after all.'

'But a privileged one.' His regard was unnerving, his slow smile even more so. 'You're shivering. I think it time we returned indoors.'

If she had shivered, it wasn't with cold, Zoe thought. He wasn't touching her in any way, yet his very closeness made her feel all churned up inside. Alexis Theodorou wasn't a man to elicit indifference in any shape or form.

'One thing I'd like making clear first,' she said. 'Who will be paying my salary from now on?'

'I will,' he answered. 'Christa no longer has any jurisdiction. However, I consider the figure she quoted to be insufficient for a position which has no set hours, so it will be increased by a third.'

'That isn't necessary,' she protested. 'I was more than happy with the original amount. After all, I enjoy a lifestyle here that many people would pay a small fortune to experience.'

Alexis gave a low laugh. 'I've never met anyone before who refused to take extra payment for their services!'

'I didn't say I was refusing, only that it isn't necessary.'

'I'll decide what is or isn't necessary.' There was more than a touch of the autocrat in that statement. 'Do you think you might sleep now?'

Zoe doubted it very much. Not with both mind and body so highly strung. The hostility she felt towards this man was in some ways a defence against his undoubted attraction. His maturity, his sheer masculinity, the very aura of power he carried about him formed an irresistible magnetism. She wouldn't be the first woman to respond to it by a long way.

She must have made some noise or nod of assent without realising it, for he put a hand on her arm to turn her back the way they had come. She could feel his fingers burning through the sleeve of her sweater, although his touch was light. He released her almost immediately to pace at her side with hands thrust into the pockets of his trousers and that same enigmatic smile on his lips, making her wonder if he had sensed her reaction and was amused by it. No doubt it *would* amuse him.

He saw her all the way to the door of her room, taking his leave with a murmured '*Kalinichta*'.

With her back against the smooth and heavy wood, Zoe took a moment or two to steady her jangling nerves before switching on a light. It was ridiculous to allow a basic physical chemistry to affect her this way. Because that was all it was. It was all she dared allow it to be. Alexis Theodorou was way outside her league.

That latter assessment was one Zoe was to remind herself of several times over the course of the next few days. Alexis spent much of his time at the company offices down in the city, but was usually at home for dinner. Zoe found his presence stimulating in a way that she knew signalled problems of a kind she could well do without. Whether he guessed how he affected her, she couldn't be sure. If he did, he was ignoring it, which was probably the best way. As an employee living as one of the family, she was in a privileged but none the less menial position. Hardly worthy of more than a passing attention.

'I'm glad Leda Kazantzi isn't at home,' declared Sofia with feeling one evening after Alexis had departed to take care of one or two pressing matters, as he had put it. 'She thinks she should have all his attention. It will be even worse if he marries her and she is here all the time.'

The two of them were relaxing for a while beneath the loggia covering one end of the paved terrace, prior to going to bed. She should have known, thought Zoe, trying to ignore the pang deep down. At thirty-four, it stood to reason that Alexis would have someone already picked out as his future bride. The only wonder was that he had waited as long as he had.

'What's she like?' she asked casually.

'Leda?' Sofia gave the matter some thought. 'She's very beautiful, of course, and of good family, but I do not care for her very much. No more than she cares for me.'

Zoe said softly, 'Alexis obviously finds her harmonic enough.'

The answer came on a resigned sigh. 'Yes.' She was silent for a moment, then her expression altered. 'We forgot to ask him about our plan for tomorrow.'

Zoe bit back the caustic rejoinder. No matter what the emotional effect Alexis might have on her, it didn't alter the fact that having to seek his prior approval of any venture they might wish to undertake was both galling and ridiculous. What harm could the two of them possibly come to together?

'He went to the office, didn't he?' she said, pressing herself to her feet in sudden resolution. 'I'll go and see him right now.'

'He may not be pleased to be interrupted,' warned Sofia, looking uncertain. 'Perhaps in the morning...'

'There's every chance that he'll be gone before we get down, as he has been this last couple of mornings,' Zoe reminded her. 'If we want to see the Acropolis before the crowds start arriving, we'll need to leave by seven-thirty ourselves. Otherwise we'll be stuck in traffic half the morning.' She hesitated, viewing the younger girl questioningly. 'You're sure *you* want to visit the sites? You're not just doing it because you think it's what I want? I mean, I have seen them all before.'

Sofia smiled. 'I am sure. It is a long time since I was last on the Acropolis.'

Zoe returned the smile. 'I'll be back in a moment or two.'

The door to the study was firmly closed. She tapped on it with reservation, unsurprised by the curtness of the invitation to enter.

Alexis was on the telephone. He signalled to her to come on in as she hesitated in the doorway, rounded off his conversation in Greek too swiftly spoken for her to even attempt to translate, apart from the *kalinichta* at the end, and replaced the receiver.

'I'm sorry to intrude,' she said. 'If I'd known you were on the phone...'

'I'd almost finished the call,' he returned. 'It's of no matter.' He studied her face, an odd expression in his eyes. 'You wished to ask me something?'

'Just to say that we—Sofia and I, that is—would like to spend the day in Athens tomorrow, if that's all right?'

There was irony in his faint smile. 'And if I say no?'

Zoe stiffened involuntarily. 'Then we wouldn't be going, obviously. Is there any particular reason why you should say no?'

'None that I can think of at present,' came the smooth reply. 'I was interested only in your reaction.' He gave her no time to respond. 'You intend visiting the Plaka?'

'No, the Acropolis and the Agora. Plus anything else we have time for before lunch.'

'You've never visited the sites before?'

'Several times,' she admitted. 'But never enough. Sofia is eager to see them again too. We thought of going early in order to avoid the crowds as much as possible.'

'A good idea,' he agreed. 'In fact, we can all of us drive in to the city together, and I'll pick you up again in the afternoon. Perhaps later we might even pay this visit to the Plaka which you were both so eager to make. I'd be happier if you didn't go out together in the evening without escort.' He raised a mocking eyebrow at her. 'You look surprised.'

'I am,' she admitted. 'I didn't expect you to agree so easily.'

'You mean you anticipated the opposition you find so stirring to your English blood. I'm sorry to deprive you of the need for confrontation. After this, you no longer need to seek my approval for any day-to-day activity you may conceive. Although I'd naturally expect to be consulted over anything out of the ordinary.'

'Why the sudden change of mind?' asked Zoe bemusedly. 'Only a few days ago you were on the verge of having me thrown out on my ear!'

His lips twitched. 'No Greek would treat a woman so, whatever the provocation. I had to be assured of your qualities before I surrendered my sister into your keeping. She's very dear to me.'

'I'm . . . gratified.' Zoe scarcely knew what else to say. He had taken the wind completely out of her sails. She rallied to add, 'I was planning on taking a car so that we'd have transport of our own while we're there.'

'Plus all the difficulties entailed in finding parking space. The Agora is within walking distance of the Acropolis, and you can take a taxi anywhere else you might want to go. There are more than enough vehicles in Athens at any one time without adding to them unnecessarily. Any expenses you entail will be refunded, of course.'

Faced with that piece of undoubted common sense, there was little Zoe could do but agree. She was also bound to confess to a stirring of anticipation at the thought of the suggested Plaka visit. Short of upping and leaving without further ado, the attraction she felt towards Alexis was something she was going to have to live with, but at the very least she could enjoy his company on occasion.

CHAPTER THREE

BREAKFAST consisted of no more than coffee and the hoop-shaped biscuits called *koulouria*. Unaccustomed to eating very much first thing in the morning herself, and taking into account the later dinner hour, Zoe had found the lack of more substantial fare no particular hardship.

Alexis was wearing a superbly cut business suit in a dark blue, and looked every inch a man of means. She felt decidedly substandard in her simple cotton print, chosen for comfort rather than show. Dressed equally simply though far from inexpensively, Sofia was as fresh as the morning. Her eyes sparkled with anticipation of the day to come.

There were no less than five vehicles in the Mimosa garages, ranging from a low-slung Porsche through to the Mercedes sometimes chauffeured by one of the male staff, Yannis, who turned his hand cheerfully to any job that came along. There were few demarcation lines among the servants, Zoe had found. Each and every one did whatever was necessary, and without rancour. Only Artemis lived in. The others came on a daily basis.

Alexis chose to take the Range Rover. Zoe had driven it herself a couple of times since her arrival, liking the sense of security afforded by its bulk and height, though she doubted if Alexis had the same motivation. With Sofia insisting on occupying a rear seat, she had little alternative but to get into the front alongside him.

The sky was cloudless, the heat haze already shimmering the distances as they drove down through the lovely old tree-lined avenues of Kifissia to take the Athens road. Alexis said little. He seemed preoccupied. Thinking about some business deal, Zoe surmised.

Her own attention was captured by the unfolding scene ahead, the oval plateau of the Acropolis standing proud of the spreading city, crowned with the glory of ages past—the fir-clad limestone heights of Lycabettus, named after the packs of wolves that had once roamed its slopes, and the wide blue expanse of the Saronic Gulf beyond. At this hour the pall of pollution was light enough to be disregarded, though not for long, as she knew from past experience.

The main thoroughfares were already heavy with traffic, the noise clamorous. Few Greek drivers paid any attention to speed limits, tearing around in a personal safety zone assured by the worry-heads swinging in rear windows. Alexis boasted no beads, but manoeuvred with a similar dexterity to drop them at the Acropolis almost on the half-hour. He would pick them up in front of the parliament building in Syntagma Square at three-thirty, he said, so that they might all have the opportunity to return home for a change of clothing before venturing into the Plaka.

Zoe was relieved to hear it. She hadn't liked the idea of spending the whole day and evening in the same things.

There were a fair number of other early risers climbing the steep and slippery marble path to the monumental gateway of the Propylaia, but not enough as yet to disturb the peace and tranquillity of the site. Even the restorers' scaffolding failed to detract from the Parthenon's eternal beauty, the sheer impact of those soaring columns.

When first constructed, Zoe knew, all the statues and relief work would have been brightly painted, the ceilings inside extravagantly gilded. Now, all that was left was the bare marble, matured from white to pale gold. In many ways it was a blessing to be banned from too close an approach. Distance hid the cracks and crumbling caused by modern-day life.

At this hour, she found it possible to move with ease through all the rooms of the museum, to linger unjostled before the statue of the Kritian Boy and admire the fluid lines of his naked body without having her interest misconstrued. She could have spent the whole morning in there, but that would hardly have been fair on Sofia.

Emerging into the open air again, looking out over the city spread below, she thought that no matter how many times she came here she would never tire of this scene. Marred though it was in parts by the blocks of concrete and brick that passed for modern architecture, it still had such tremendous visual impact. The sense of history was overwhelming. From a hill opposite the Acropolis, St Paul had stood to preach his new religion.

'The tourist coaches are beginning to arrive,' observed Sofia, looking down to the avenue running so sadly close to the Odeon of Herodes Atticus. 'Should we not leave now before it becomes too busy?'

Zoe agreed with resignation. The atmosphere would be ruined, anyway, once the crowds took over. There was always another day. After standing for almost two and a half thousand years, the Parthenon was hardly going to crumble away overnight.

'Are you sure you don't mind visiting the Agora?' she asked on the way down. 'You must have been there a hundred times before.'

Sofia shook her head. 'Only a very few. And of course I do not mind. I am happy to be anywhere with you, Zoe. You make everything seem so interesting!'

How anyone could live their life on the very doorstep of this home of the gods and find it no more than interesting was beyond all comprehension to Zoe. She supposed it was a fact that over-exposure could reduce even the glorious to the mundane. The Athenians themselves took their heritage for granted because it had always been there. Their day-to-day concerns lay in the hustle and bustle of the modern city.

'Perhaps some coffee first?' she suggested, knowing Sofia's love of the beverage—Greek days were punctuated by coffee breaks. They would have to find a general café, of course. The traditional *kafeneion* tended to remain an all-male domain even now. It would take someone with far more face than she would ever have to try knocking on *that* door, she acknowledged, regardless of what Alexis might think of her militant tendencies.

The ancient Greek market place looked even more like a bomb site than the last time she had visited it. All the same, it still evoked a strong sense of past times. Despite the people around, and the distant traffic noises, closing one's eyes, it was easy to imagine the way it must have been in its heyday; to visualise the money-changers, barbers, animal and food merchants; to hear the hammering of nails from the cobbler's shop, the clang of iron from the forge. It was almost a disappointment to open them again and find oneself back in the twentieth century.

The museum here was crowded by now with tour groups of various nationalities. Getting close enough to view any exhibits at all meant rubbing shoulders, elbows and sometimes more delicate parts of the anatomy with one's neighbours.

Stepping back at one point on to someone's toes, Zoe turned to direct an apologetic smile at the young fair-haired man, guessing his nationality to be either British or American. 'Sorry,' she said, 'that was clumsy of me.'

'My own fault for standing too close,' he returned. 'No harm done, anyway. You're not exactly heavy.' The blue eyes were frankly appreciative as they rested on her face beneath its riot of copper curls. 'Are you with one of the groups?'

Zoe looked around for Sofia, but failed to spot her among the milling throngs. 'No, I'm living here. For the present, anyway. You're taller than me,' she added. 'Can you see a small dark-haired girl wearing a white dress anywhere?'

'Over there, underneath the portico,' he said after a moment. 'Being harassed, by the look of it. This way.'

Zoe allowed herself to be drawn in the direction indicated, to be greeted with relief by Sofia, who had attracted the attentions of a trio of Italian students.

'Let's get out of here,' suggested their new-found friend. 'Too many bodies around for comfort.'

With the Italian trio still hovering, Zoe made no demur. 'Thanks,' she said when they were outside again in the sunshine. 'Those three looked like trouble.'

'They were making rude noises with their lips,' Sofia confirmed. 'Not very nice.' She looked at the newcomer with interest. 'Are you here on holiday?'

'No, to work,' he said. 'I only arrived yesterday, so I'm just finding my way around. I'm Paul Kenyon, by the way.'

Zoe performed return introductions, liking his clean-cut looks and casually smart appearance. Not much more than her own age, she judged.

'What kind of work?' she asked.

'Travel agent. I'm on a six-month exchange, starting after Easter. I came over early to give myself time to get orientated first. I've only visited Athens once before, and that was years ago.' He paused, looking from one to the other speculatively. 'What do you two do for a living, then?'

'Zoe is my friend,' said Sofia before the former could answer. 'She takes care of me.'

'Companion is the official term,' Zoe supplied, seeing his puzzled expression. 'Not that it's at all like a job.' The last with a smile at the younger girl. 'As Sofia just said, we've become very good friends.'

'I didn't realise there was any call this day and age,' Paul admitted. He sounded intrigued. 'You just live in like one of the family, then?'

'Zoe is my sister in all but name,' Sofia declared, bringing a warm glow to Zoe's heart. 'There is no difference between us.'

The intrigue deepened. 'Is that how your parents view it too?'

'My parents are passed away,' she acknowledged. 'There is just myself and my brother, and my older sister in England, although we have other relatives both here in Athens and other parts of Greece.' She eyed him expectantly. 'Do you have family?'

The readiness with which most Greek people were prepared to offer detailed information about themselves was balanced by an equal curiosity about others. Diffident still to a certain extent in exerting her will, Sofia was no exception to the rule when it came to probing backgrounds, Zoe had discovered. In two minutes she had established that Paul was twenty-four and came from Crawley, where he lived with his parents and two teenage sisters. He had been involved in the travel industry for the last three years.

Zoe could see no harm in agreeing to his suggestion that the three of them go and have a coffee together, and Sofia certainly showed no objection. They found a back-street café within walking distance of the Agora, and spent a pleasant half-hour or so in idle chat.

Here, just a stone's throw away from the traffic-thronged main streets, the atmosphere was so different.

Flowering plants trained on trellises festooned every cornice, ledge and balcony within sight, overlaying the smell of sulphur dioxide with the scents of jasmine and lavender. A short distance away, out in front of a small shop, a group of men were gathered about a portable television supported on an orange crate, intent, to the exclusion of everything else about them, on whatever it was they were watching, while just beyond an old woman dressed from head to toe in unrelieved black swept the step of her home with an old-fashioned broom. It was like being caught up in a temporary time-warp.

'What are you thinking of doing with the rest of the day?' asked Paul on a far from casual note when they finally made a move. 'I'd be really grateful if I could tag along for a while. Perhaps we could have lunch together?'

Sofia showed no hesitation in accepting that suggestion either. Paul was a new friend, and she obviously found his company stimulating. Whether Alexis would approve of such an informal acquaintanceship was a matter for speculation, but she could hardly tell him no, Zoe decided. There was no harm, surely, in extending the hand of friendship to a fellow countryman?

All of them enjoyed the following couple of hours. Paul proved himself quite knowledgeable on historic detail, and a regular devotee of Greek mythology. They finished up eventually at one of the open-air restaurants in Syntagma Square for lunch, not because it was one of the better places at which to eat, but because it was one of the few that still had tables unoccupied at a time when most of Athens was of the same mind.

Apart from the traffic, which never seemed to decrease, the whole pace of life slowed down for two or three hours every afternoon. Zoe had always considered the idea of a lengthy and leisurely break in the hottest part of the day a particularly sensible one. Better to work later into the evening when the sun had lost its strength and humidity was lowering.

With its shady orange trees and fountains, the central island was an oasis hemmed in by tall new buildings and elderly hotels, all dominated by the great fawn-coloured edifice which had been the old royal palace and was now the parliament building. There was a story, said Paul, that the site for the royal residence had been selected by the young King Otho himself via a process of hanging up hunks of meat in various parts of the town to see where maggots were slowest to hatch, but he didn't personally believe it.

It was his suggestion that they share a bottle of *retsina* with their moussaka. Having developed a taste for the resinous wine in the past, Zoe watched with sly amusement as he took his first sip, unsurprised to see his nose wrinkle.

'It takes a bit of perseverance,' she agreed.

'Plus a fair streak of masochism!' came the wry comment.

Sofia looked puzzled. 'What,' she asked, 'do you mean?'

'It was a joke,' Zoe explained. 'It's only——' She broke off abruptly, eyes riveted on the man getting out of the car which had just drawn in to the kerbside some dozen or so yards away. 'It's Alexis,' she said in sudden consternation. 'What on earth is the time?'

He came straight over to their table, lip curling in distaste as he surveyed their immediate surroundings. A bit touristy, Zoe had to admit, but there was no need for him to make his opinion quite so obvious. The glance he gave Paul was far from friendly too.

'I saw you from the car as I was on my way round to where I told you to wait for me,' he said pointedly. 'Why do you eat at such a place?'

'Because this was where we happened to be when it came to lunchtime,' Zoe returned with what equability she could muster.

'We were hungry,' said Sofia on a placatory note, 'and the moussaka is good. This is Paul's first time in Athens, Alexis. He is English too.'

Smile easy, Paul came to his feet. 'The name's Kenyon. You must be Sofia's brother. *Khero poli*, Kyrie Theodorou.'

Alexis shook the proffered hand perfunctorily, unimpressed by the badly accented Greek. 'You're a friend of Zoe's?' he enquired.

Paul laughed. 'I am now, I hope. And of Sofia's too. I've felt like a million dollars this morning, squiring two beautiful girls around the town!'

'I'm sure you have.' Alexis's tone was silky. 'You're here as a tourist?'

'No, to work. At a travel agency.' He named the one, starting to look just a little uncertain at the lack of cordiality in the other's manner. 'We bumped into each other at the Agora—or at least Zoe bumped into me.' The last with a swift smile in her direction. 'The hand of fate!' His glance came back to the older man. 'We just sort of took it from there.'

'As I,' came the rejoinder, 'will take it from here.' Dark eyes met green, the displeasure unconcealed. 'You've finished your meal?'

It was as much statement as question. Zoe felt resentment flicker to life. 'As near as makes no difference, I suppose,' she returned coolly.

Paul made a sudden movement, almost of protest, as both girls rose. 'I was hoping we could meet up again now that we've got to know one another,' he said to Zoe. 'In your free time, of course.'

Aware of Alexis's drawn brows and obvious disapproval, she gave the resentment free rein. 'That would be nice. Perhaps I could telephone you and arrange something? Where are you staying?'

From his wry expression as he scribbled down the address and telephone number on a scrap of paper, it was apparent that Paul took the suggestion as polite evasion. Alexis waited in silence until she had put the paper in her purse, then indicated that they should take their leave.

Sofia seemed somewhat dispirited herself as they went to the waiting car. Still standing by the table they had vacated, Paul gave a wave when they pulled away from the kerb into the stream of traffic. Zoe returned the gesture with intent.

'Is it your custom to form such immediate familiarity with strangers?' Alexis demanded tautly.

'Meaning men in particular?' she asked, and heard him draw in a hard breath.

'You know exactly what I mean!'

Zoe kept her eyes on the thronging traffic ahead. Physical attraction withstanding, she had no intention of allowing him to browbeat her over a simple friendly gesture.

'We were hardly in any danger,' she declared. 'There were plenty of people around the whole time. Not that I'd consider Paul in the light of a potential rapist, in any case. Like me, he's here to work.' She tagged on swiftly, 'Not that I think of mine as just another job, by any means.'

'I'm very glad to hear it.' The irony was heavy. 'So you won't be telephoning this Paul.'

She doubted it herself, but saw no reason to tell him so. 'I didn't say that. After all, we're both English—and we do seem to have quite a lot in common.'

'Zoe is entitled to have time of her own, Alexis,' said Sofia from the back. She sounded a little dejected. 'I cannot expect to take all of it.'

Zoe turned to her remorsefully. 'You mustn't feel like that. I love being with you! If I didn't I wouldn't still be here, believe me!'

Sofia returned the smile, though with some slight reservation still lingering. 'You are still entitled to take time to yourself. There should be some arrangement—yes, Alexis?'

Zoe was beginning to regret that she had ever started this. She felt no sense of restriction in the sense to which Sofia was referring. This wasn't the kind of job where one either wanted or expected to clock on and off at regular times.

'We'll discuss it,' said Alexis, before she could come up with any further assurance. His tone was clipped, his attitude noticeably cooler than it had been these past two or three days. 'Sofia is right, of course.'

Sitting back in her seat, Zoe felt anything but happy about it all, although she realised that Sofia did indeed have a point. They couldn't spend all day and every day for a whole year in one another's pockets.

They reached the villa in a great deal less time than it had taken to make the same length of journey that morning. Alexis gave the two of them until five o'clock to prepare for the evening's activities. Having showered, Zoe chose a short-sleeved suit in white linen as the smartest outfit in her wardrobe, teaming it with a sleeveless, scoop-necked blouse in palest amber, and low-heeled sandals.

She was dressing as much to please Alexis as herself, she conceded wryly, viewing her appearance. Not that it mattered in the long run how she looked. He might have relaxed formality to a certain degree, but she was still an employee, subject to his wishes; he had made that position clear this afternoon.

Whether she would telephone Paul or not, she hadn't fully decided. Senseless, perhaps, to make an issue of something she didn't really care all that much about. If she needed time to herself for anything, then it could surely be arranged as and when. Until such time, she was more than content to go on as they were.

The Plaka district of Athens climbed the northern slopes of the Acropolis. Zoe loved the maze of streets with their numerous small shops and smell of spitted meat and spices, the miniature Byzantine chapels and old city houses. She had stayed in the Plaka on her last visit to the city after gaining her degree. The hotel had been small and simple, but had afforded a superb view of the Acropolis from her bedroom. There was little culture to be found in the general run of doubtful antiques, tourist-aimed souvenirs and 'I love Greece' T-shirts, she was the first to acknowledge, but a great deal of entertainment.

That Sofia shared her opinion was more than apparent. She couldn't have enough of it all. Alexis indulged her eager exploration of each and every shop, with good grace. Casually clad in white trousers and dark green shirt, he drew many an admiring female eye. He had to be aware of the attention, Zoe was sure, yet he showed no sign of having noticed.

'You're very quiet,' he commented at one point when Sofia was engaged in looking at leather coats which she couldn't possibly want and certainly didn't need. 'Are you bored?'

'Not at all,' she denied. 'This is my favourite part of all Athens—modern Athens, that is.'

'You don't find it too crowded and busy?'

'It's part and parcel,' she said. 'I like the atmosphere. It might be a bit touristy, but it still has a lot to offer. A rest from breathing in the traffic fumes, for instance.'

'There is that,' he agreed. 'Athens is fast becoming a no-go area for anyone who values his or her health—

although no more than many other Common Market capitals I've visited.'

'You obviously take a very active part in company affairs,' she commented lightly. 'More so than many in your position, I'd think.'

The dark head inclined. 'Money doesn't excuse a man from hard work, it just excuses him from some particular kinds of hard work. I've no intention of leaving matters in the hands of my uncle and cousins, much as they would like it.'

'You mean the whole family is involved?'

He lifted a brow. 'You find that strange?'

'As a matter of fact, I find it highly commendable,' she said truthfully. 'I admire the way Greek families stick together.'

'Like glue,' he agreed a little drily. He took her arm as a passer-by jostled her, moving her further in towards the wall of the little colour-washed house which opened directly on to the street. The hand stayed where it was, lightly supporting her elbow, his expression difficult to define as he studied her face. 'Our ways are very different,' he observed. 'I must remember to make allowances. What do you plan to do with your life after this year is over?'

Zoe's voice sounded husky. 'As I said before, go back to teaching. Or I might take the opportunity to do some travelling. There's a whole lot of world out there. I want to see as much of it as I can before I die.'

'You should have no thoughts of death at your age,' he admonished. 'You have a lifetime to live.' His tone altered subtly. 'And to love.'

Zoe's heart jerked painfully. He was playing with her, she told herself, finding a passing amusement in this English girl who made her response to him so obvious. She forced a light rejoinder. 'I thought you were of the opinion that love was an unnecessary emotion?'

'I said it wasn't essential in marriage, not that I was against the feeling itself.' His voice was soft, the very quality of it tingling her skin. 'Have you ever been in love?'

'You asked me that the other night,' she got out.

'What we talked of the other night was to do with lust, not love,' he denied. 'I repeat, have you ever really loved a man?'

She felt herself drowning in the dark eyes, and made a supreme effort to cast off the spell. 'Not in any depth.'

His gaze sharpened. 'But you've imagined yourself in love at some time?'

'Hasn't everyone?' The flippancy in her voice was deliberate. 'It's what makes the world go round!' She sobered to add succinctly, 'If you're thinking I might lead Sofia into viewing things my way, you don't need to worry. I've no intention of trying to change her ideas.'

'Apart from where they concern her readiness for marriage, perhaps?'

Her chin lifted. 'She's already of the same opinion herself.'

'Then you've discussed it with her?'

'Only to discover how she really feels about it.'

'And?' he prompted.

'I think she'd do whatever it took to please you, even suffer Orestes Antoniou for a husband. If you care anything at all for her feelings, you'll tell her she doesn't have anything to worry about where he's concerned.' She hurried on, determined to get it all off her chest before the spark she could see growing in his eyes turned into a blaze. 'He's not good enough for her, in any case!'

Surprisingly the spark turned to amusement. 'The Antonious would be most interested to hear your opinion of their standing.'

'I'm not talking about the family as a whole,' she defended, 'just Orestes himself. I'd say his eyes were more on the dowry Sofia would bring with her. Some people are born avaricious.'

The amusement was replaced by some other expression less easily distinguished. 'You place a lot of reliance on your instincts, Zoe. Do they never let you down?'

It was the very first time he had used her Christian name. It sounded strange on his lips. 'I wouldn't say they were infallible,' she acknowledged. 'Only I doubt if I'm wrong in this instance. Orestes doesn't look at Sofia the way a man should look at the girl he wants for herself alone.'

'And which way is that?' Alexis insisted. 'You've seen this look for yourself?'

'On occasion. I have a girlfriend back home,' she improvised, 'whose fiancé looks at her as if there were no other girl on earth to match her.'

'And how does she look back at him?'

He was mocking her, Zoe knew, but she refused to be deterred by the knowledge. 'Much the same way. They're in love.'

'Which brings us back to where we began,' he said. 'As to Sofia...' The pause seemed to go on forever, ending in a reserved, 'I'll think long and hard on the subject.'

'For her sake, I hope so.' Zoe added quickly, 'Isn't it time we went to find her?'

'We know where she is,' he said. 'She'll hardly wander away while we stand here in full view.'

It was with a mingling of relief and regret that Zoe saw the young Greek girl emerge at that moment from among the hanging racks of coats and jackets. Alexis took his hand from her arm as she made a move away from the wall, turning without haste to view his sister's empty hands.

'You decided against buying?'

'I was only looking,' Sofia claimed. 'I have no need of a coat.'

Especially not one from here, Zoe surmised. Sofia's wardrobe owed much to Italian and French manufacture and design. The simple little cotton and silk knit skirt and top she was wearing now was imported, and had no doubt cost the earth. Alexis was generosity itself when it came to anything money could buy, but she wondered just how much Sofia really meant to him. If he continued to see Orestes Antoniou as a prospective husband for her, the answer had to be very little.

CHAPTER FOUR

NEON lights flickered into life as the evening advanced, and the sound of music began to filter out from tavernas and bars. More and more people appeared on the streets. Tourists, for the main part, Zoe judged, catching snatches of German and French and what she thought might be Swedish.

Easter in Greece was dated by the Orthodox calendar, and generally fell about a month later than the Western celebration. With just over a week to go, the city was starting to fill up with a vengeance. Sofia had been right in saying that Zoe would be lucky to find reasonably priced accommodation going spare anywhere at short notice.

The taverna to which Alexis eventually took them for the promised meal was on one of the lesser-used thoroughfares. It had a small roof garden, profuse in spilling flower-boxes and set with tables and chairs to seat a dozen or so people. From here there was a wonderful view of the Parthenon, its ancient pillars floodlit against a sky of midnight blue. One of these evenings, Zoe promised herself, she would attend the Son et Lumière conducted from the Pnyx.

For someone who visited the Plaka only under protest, Alexis certainly knew the right places, she reflected, enjoying the savoury balls of meat and rice, served in a delicious egg and lemon sauce, which she had chosen as her main course. *Youvazlakia*, the dish was called, which was a mouthful in itself! She would certainly have to remember it for future reference.

'You have a better appetite tonight,' Alexis was moved to remark when she cleared her plate. He poured more of the excellent Naoussa wine for them all, added, 'Perhaps you might like to visit a *zakharoplasteion* for *baklava* and coffee to finish?'

Zoe shook her head. The sweet, sticky cakes held little appeal for her at any time, much less now. 'I'm full, thank you.'

'I love *baklava*!' exclaimed Sofia. 'I'd like some, please, Alexis.' Her sudden laugh was pure delight. 'There! I'm learning to speak English properly now!'

'That,' he said, 'is a contradiction in terms. You're learning to speak colloquial English.'

'Do you object?' asked Zoe quickly.

He shrugged. 'Why should I object when I myself use the informal mode?' Catching her faint smile, he gave her a quizzical look. 'You wouldn't agree?'

'I think you speak excellent English,' she hastened to assure him. 'Far, far better than I'll ever speak Greek. I can't even get the sound right.'

'It will come,' he said. 'You have plenty of time.'

She had a bare year, but she wasn't quibbling. If nothing else, she intended to be reasonably fluent by the time she left the country.

It was gone eleven-thirty when they finally arrived back at the villa. Still early by Greek standards, though Sofia proclaimed herself too tired to stay up any longer.

Zoe was torn between two fires when Alexis suggested a nightcap before they too retired. On the one hand was her reluctance for the evening to end, on the other her growing awareness of piling up a certain heartache for herself if she wasn't careful. The attention Alexis had paid her tonight meant little, different though his manner had been from that which he had displayed earlier when she had displeased him. An amusing diversion for a man of his kind, nothing more.

He solved the problem by taking her agreement for granted. Seated on one of the comfortable squashy sofas in the smaller of the two *salonia*, she steeled herself for the fleeting contact with his fingertips as she took the glass of brandy from him. Vintage, she reckoned, taking a sip of the golden liquid. Excellent, anyway.

'You approve?' he asked.

'Very much,' she declared. 'Though I'd have been quite happy with Metaxa.'

'It *is* Metaxa,' he said. 'The very finest. I'm very patriotic in my tastes.' His gaze moved over her in open commendation. 'You look very elegant tonight.'

'It's quite an old outfit,' she deprecated automatically, and saw his mouth take on a slant.

'Why is it that English women find compliments so difficult to accept?'

'I don't know,' she admitted. 'Something to do with not being all that used to them, I suppose.'

'It's true then that Englishmen fail to appreciate their womenfolk?'

She laughed. 'More a case, I suppose, of not being given to putting it into words. The strong, silent type, that's the ideal image.'

'The kind of image you prefer yourself?'

'It depends,' she hedged, 'on the man. Some are suited to that role, others...'

'Others?' he prompted as she allowed her voice to trail away.

'Are... different, that's all.' She registered the slow smile with a fluttering of her pulses, half wishing now that she had resisted temptation and gone straight to bed. Alexis was taking this game of his a little too far.

'The Americans would call that a "cop-out",' he said. 'Tell me, to which role am I suited?'

'Provocateur,' she retorted, drawn despite herself by the glint in the dark eyes.

He hadn't taken a seat himself. Standing there, glass in hand, and that deceptively lazy smile on his lips, he caused Zoe's heart to thud suddenly and painfully against her ribcage.

'The provocation,' he said softly, 'isn't one-sided. I've been aware of it since the very first moment we met. The other night, in the garden, I wanted to make love to you—as I do right now. You want it too. I see it in your eyes.'

Her heart had quickened its beat to a point where it was in danger of breaking through the wall of her chest. She put down her glass with a hand that trembled, unable to credit that she was hearing him right. 'I think it's time I said goodnight.'

'Because I say what is on both our minds?' Alexis was smiling still. 'I feel the same attraction for you that you feel for me. I see no point in pretence.'

'Apparently not.' Her voice sounded thick. 'Is it a condition of my continuing employment that I admit to this ... attraction, and act accordingly?'

'An enhancement, perhaps.'

'I see.' She came jerkily to her feet. 'Then the answer is no!'

'The answer to what?' he asked without change of inflexion. 'I asked nothing of you as yet.'

The searing anger in her was as much a product of disillusionment as righteous indignation. 'You've made it more than obvious what it is that you want. You don't waste any time, do you, *kyrie*? Three days! I just can't believe it!'

'I find it difficult to believe myself,' he admitted, unmoved by the searing attack. 'I fought against it too for all of several minutes after you left me that first afternoon, but to no avail. You sat there, defying me, your hair like newly minted copper and eyes full of green fire, and I wanted you as I've rarely wanted a woman before.'

'Then too bad you're going to be disappointed!' Zoe was hurting too much to think about what she was saying. 'I'll be leaving first thing in the morning.'

'With no thought for Sofia?' He gave her no time to reply. 'You convinced me of her need for greater freedom. If you abandon her now, she'll be back to where she was before.'

Zoe bit her lip. 'Meaning you'd make sure of it?'

'Meaning that it would be difficult to find another companion whom I could trust to have the same regard for her that you have yourself. As to your own needs, you said only the other night that they were no different from those of the male.'

She had said a great deal too much the other night, Zoe reflected painfully. Not really so surprising that he should have taken her at her word. He was unaccustomed to being turned down, for certain. The Alexis Theodorous of this world were used to having whatever they wanted for the taking. If it weren't for Sofia, she wouldn't even be hesitating, but how could she possibly explain her reasons for such an abrupt departure without telling her the truth? The last thing she would want was to destroy her belief in her brother's integrity.

'I was generalising,' she said desperately. 'You're putting me in an impossible position! Don't you care about anything but what *you* want?'

His mouth slanted again. 'There are certain emotions which tend to take precedence over others in all of us. Do you think me incapable of recognising desire in a woman? You vibrate with it whenever I touch you.'

She was vibrating right now. With anger, she told herself, and knew that wasn't wholly true. His very arrogance was a part of his mesmeric attraction. She had given him the impression herself that she was of open mind where sexual freedom was concerned; admitting that she had been talking through her hat was going to be mortifying, to say the least.

'I think you've—misunderstood me,' she began haltingly. 'I'm not what I might have seemed to be. What I said the other night wasn't meant to be taken seriously. Not in any personal sense.'

'You claimed the right to enjoy sexual relationships without censure,' Alexis quoted. 'I grant you that right.' The dark eyes were giving off sparks. 'I think it's time I showed you how the Greeks make love to a woman.'

Zoe backed up a step as he moved towards her, to be brought up short by the edge of the sofa. She put up a hand in a futile staying gesture, and saw the olive-skinned features go rigid for a moment before Alexis took hold of her wrist and drew her forcibly to him.

'Be careful how you make that sign to a Greek unless you intend to offer him insult,' he advised softly.

Zoe stiffened under the demanding pressure of his lips, fighting the instincts flooding through her at the sheer impact. The scent of him filled her nostrils, the feel of him her every fibre. He was so hard, so strong, so utterly and completely male.

Her control began slipping, bit by bit, allowing her lips to soften beneath his, to move in unison, her whole body to come into vibrant contact. He slid a hand up underneath her hair to tangle it in the thickness, bringing her closer still with a firm pressure at the centre of her back.

She had never known so swift and consuming a desire. It swept over her like a riptide, urging her to go with it, to forget about resistance, to experience the full sensual ecstasy that she knew this man could provide.

Without taking his lips wholly from hers, Alexis pressed her down slowly but surely on to the sofa, lifting her legs over his own as he sank to a seat beside her.

The touch of his hand at her breast was like fire; she wanted those long and tensile fingers on her bare skin. It took every ounce of will-power she could dredge up to pull her back from the brink.

'Stop it,' she whispered. 'Please, Alexis!'

'Why?' he asked thickly. 'You want me to go on. I can feel it in you.' He lifted his head to look at her, eyes smouldering like live coals. 'You want me the same way that I want you. Can you deny it?'

'Not like this!' The words were dragged from her. 'I'm not some cheap little pick-up, ready to go to bed with any man!'

'I am not,' he declared, 'just *any* man!'

'No,' she answered, 'you're my employer. That makes it even worse. What kind of suitable companion for Sofia would I be if I did what you're asking?'

'They are two different things,' he said. 'I trust you with Sofia because I believe you really care for her. That doesn't mean that I can't want you for myself.' His voice roughened. 'Are you trying to deny the way you responded to me just now?'

Zoe made herself hold his gaze, made herself answer honestly. 'I could hardly do that.'

'Then why,' he asked, 'do you not follow your heart?'

'Because it isn't my heart that's involved.' It was already a lie, and she knew it, but she had no intention of letting him know it too. He wanted her physically, not emotionally. Once he'd had his way, the interest would be gone. She wasn't equipped to carry on afterwards as though nothing had happened between them.

'The heart,' he declared, 'is always involved!' He brought up a hand to trace the shape of her mouth with his fingertip, tremoring her stomach muscles and drawing an involuntary gasp as he followed the line of her jaw with the same slow and delicate caress to find the pulse-spot behind the lobe of her ear.

Eyes closed, Zoe felt her senses swimming, her will-power fading, her body stirring to the practised touch. When Alexis bent his head and took the tender lobe between his teeth she could hardly bear it, yet nor could she bear him to stop.

She slid her fingers through the thickness of his hair, loving the strong, wiry texture of it, then down and over the broad shoulders, feeling the muscle ripple as he drew her closer. This time the kiss was gentler at first, lips teasing, driving her frantic with sheer sensation. This time it was she who sought deeper, unable to hold back, feeling the surging response in him.

She made no sound of protest when he removed her jacket, thrilling to the feel of his fingers caressing her bare arms. Her skin prickled as if all the nerve-endings were exposed when he slid his hand up the back of her loose top to seek the fastening of her flimsy brassière. She was beyond objecting now to anything he did; she wanted whatever he wanted.

Her whole body tensed as he freed the solitary clip and found her bare breast. The nipple was already standing hard and proud. A moan was jerked from her lips as he brushed his thumb across the taut flesh. His hand was so wonderfully sensitive; she arched instinctively to allow him full play.

When he lifted her blouse and lowered his head to take one tender nub into his mouth her insides turned fluid. She opened her mouth on a silent scream at the exquisite agony inflicted by lip and tongue and teeth. Not rough, not gentle either, but somewhere subtly and erotically between, pulsing her blood through her veins like liquid fire. She scarcely knew whether to be glad or sorry when he lifted his head again and splayed his fingers to cup the whole tender fullness in his palm.

'So beautiful,' he murmured. 'As I knew you would be when I saw you emerge like Aphrodite from the water.

I want to know every inch of you, *agapi mou*. The way only a man can know a woman. I want to feel you tremble beneath me as I take you, to hear you cry out in ecstasy. But not here, like this. Not when there are places more conducive within reach.'

He placed a last fleeting kiss on her lips, then pulled down her blouse and moved her legs away so that he could get to his feet, looking down at her with the fire still smouldering in his eyes. 'Come.'

Zoe stayed where she was, only now beginning to appreciate just how far she had allowed things to go. The desire wasn't dead by any means; she could feel the heat of it radiating through her. Only the shame and debasement were stronger right now. Three days! That was all it had taken. How could she justify her near-total surrender to such a cheap emotion?

Alexis's brows drew together. 'What is it?'

Her lips felt as stiff as boards. It was an effort to force the words out at all. 'I'm sorry. I shouldn't have allowed things to get out of hand. I can't go through with this.'

'Why not?' he demanded. 'Because I ask that we go somewhere else? We can stay right here if you prefer it.'

'It isn't that.' She pushed herself upright, unsurprised to find her legs like jelly. It took even more of an effort to stand firm and face up to what was surely coming. Bare feet away, Alexis regarded her with hardened, narrowed gaze. She drew in a steadying breath before continuing. 'I prefer not to carry on at all. In fact, I'd prefer to forget that anything happened.'

There was a sudden blanking out of expression in the hard-boned face. 'Is that so? And if I decide otherwise?'

The anger sweeping through Zoe was a defence against the sheer mortification. 'Then you'll just have to whistle! It's bad enough as it is without going any further. All right, so I got carried away for a while. You're not exactly inexperienced when it comes to . . . to . . .'

'Making love to a woman?' he supplied drily as she sought around for the words. 'I doubt if you'd have responded the way you did if I *were* inexperienced.' He made a brusque gesture. 'I hadn't judged you the kind to play this sort of game with a man.'

'It was no game!' she flung at him. 'I couldn't help myself. That should satisfy your *perifania*, at least. If you hadn't stopped when you did, and given me a chance to think straight, it would probably have all been over by now, so if you're going to blame anyone for the fact that you didn't get further blame yourself!'

'I can assure you,' he said tautly, 'that it would *not* have been all over by now. We had only just begun. Would you have preferred me to strip you of your clothing here and now—to take you on the floor as if you were some common whore?'

The searing tone brought hot colour racing under her skin. 'Isn't that the way you see me, anyway?' she asked, low-toned. 'An easy lay, it's called where I come from. If it's of any satisfaction, I'm deeply ashamed of the way I've behaved tonight. I lost my head, and there's no excuse for it.'

For a moment or two the anger continued to hold sway in Alexis's eyes, before giving way to a somewhat sardonic humour. 'I can find some satisfaction in considering myself cause enough,' he said. 'As to the other, I see you as a very beautiful and desirable young woman with a strength of will I can admire even while I regret it. I still want you—perhaps the more so because you challenge me this way.'

'I'm not trying to challenge you,' Zoe denied. 'Really I'm not!'

'But you do.' There was resolution in the line of his mouth. 'You'd have little regard for a man who took you at your word when he knows full well that it isn't what you really want. Have your way tonight, if you must, but don't expect forbearance on my part after this. The next time we make love it will be wholly and completely, and because you want it too.' He paused there, assessing her reaction. 'You disbelieve me?'

She made a helpless little movement of her hands. 'I'm not sure what to think.'

'Then don't think,' he said. 'Just accept that what each of us feels for the other is one and the same.'

Not quite, she thought hollowly. Not nearly, in fact. What she felt for Alexis went deeper than mere physical hunger, and was going to go deeper still if she allowed herself to go along with him.

She had to think, and think hard, about staying on at Mimosa, because there was no doubt that he meant every word he had said. If she did stay, she would be more or less inviting an affair that could well leave her devastated. And for what? Could the kind of fulfilment he offered be worth the regret that was sure to follow?

She made a valiant effort to ignore the small voice that whispered yes.

Alexis made no move when she roused herself like a sleepwalker to reach for the jacket he had tossed so carelessly over the sofa-arm.

'I'll say goodnight, then,' she managed with creditable control of both voice and limb.

'So it seems.' He sounded remarkably unemotional about it. 'I intend to have you, Zoe, make no mistake about that. We belong together, you and I.'

But for how long? she wondered numbly. A man like Alexis could take his pleasure and go on his way unscathed, but she wasn't capable of such a short-term outlook. She had already been more than halfway in love with him before this happened, if the truth were known. If she gave in to the fire he had lit in her tonight it would consume her.

She made her escape on legs that threatened to give way underneath her. The whole situation was impossible. She had to go. Of course she had to go! How could she stay?

Rising at seven, after a restless night struggling with that question, she was no nearer a convincing decision. Sofia eyed her in some concern when they met on the terrace for breakfast.

'You look far from yourself,' she observed. 'Are you feeling unwell?'

Zoe forced a smile and a shrug. 'Just a bit off-colour, that's all. Nothing to worry about. What do you fancy doing today?'

'I thought that we might visit with my aunt in Psychiko. It's time that I made some effort.'

'Do your relatives visit here?' asked Zoe curiously.

'Not unless Alexis wishes it. Sometimes he arranges a gathering of all the family together, but we are not as close-knit as some. There is envy because of his position and wealth.'

'You mean some of them are less wealthy?'

'*Ne.*' She made an apologetic little gesture. 'I mean, yes.'

'We don't have to speak English all the time,' Zoe responded. 'My Greek isn't going to improve without practice.' She added carefully, '*Boro na tilephonisso stin Anglia, parakalo*?'

Sofia clapped her hands. 'Of course you must. Alexis has gone, so you can use the telephone in his office for privacy. Your parents must be anxious for more news of you.'

They would be more than anxious if they knew the kind of situation she was in, thought Zoe wryly. Not that she planned on telling them. This was something she had to sort out for herself, although how, she still wasn't sure.

Her stomach did a flip at the memory of last night's excesses. Had she really been so overpowered that she couldn't have stopped Alexis from doing the things he had done? Her objections had been so weak, so obviously phoney. He had known from the start exactly how she felt.

She supposed she should be grateful that he hadn't seen fit to make her face up to her duplicity there and then, although force was hardly his style. She doubted very much that he'd ever had to use any form of persuasion before. Many women would probably consider themselves highly complimented to be desired with such intensity by Alexis Theodorou.

Unfortunately, she wasn't one of them. Lust was lust, whichever way you spelled it out. All he really wanted was her body to use until he grew tired of it. A pity he hadn't been born in the days when slave girls had provided such services on order. He would have been in his element!

There was some degree of unfairness in that assessment, she knew. His approach had been as much in response to the vibrations she was giving out as his own desire. There was always the chance that he might even have thought better of it all in the cold light of day.

Determinedly, she shelved the problem. There would be time enough later to face it again if need be.

She waited until eight-thirty British time before placing the call home. Her mother answered, delighted to hear her voice.

'It's a very bad line,' she complained after asking the usual questions. 'You sound so distant. It's raining again here. Need I ask what the weather is like where you are?'

'Fine, dry and warm,' Zoe confirmed. 'Is Dad OK?'

'Yes, but he misses you. He left half an hour ago to try and escape the thick of the morning traffic. It gets worse!'

'Not a patch on Athens. It's nose-to-tail all day here!'

'You don't attempt to drive in it yourself, do you?' her mother asked on an anxious note. 'The wrong side of the road, too!'

'There's a chauffeur to take us anywhere we want to go.' Zoe considered the prevarication excusable if it stopped her mother from worrying about her on that score. Did she but know it, the busy roads were her least concern. 'No need to lift a finger, in fact,' she added cheerfully. 'I'd better finish now, Mom. The line is getting worse. I'll phone again next week.'

A wave of homesickness swept over her for a moment or two when she replaced the receiver. If she had stayed where she belonged, she wouldn't be in this mess. And mess, it was. Alexis wasn't going to back out on his declared intention; he saw her refusal merely as a challenge to be overcome. There was every chance that he would overcome it too, if she gave him an opportunity to repeat last night's attack on her senses.

So make sure there is no further opportunity, the voice of reason supplied. If she avoided being alone with him, he could hardly make any move. She thrust aside the treacherous temptation to let matters take their course. No good could come of that kind of indulgence.

The trip to Psychiko was made before lunch. In her late fifties, and speaking no English, Ariadne Theodorou showed little pleasure on seeing her niece, but launched almost immediately into a fervent and obviously heartfelt tirade. It was time, Zoe gathered from what few words she could grasp, that Alexis himself made some acknowledgement of the debt owed to his uncle and two cousins with an increase in salary for all three.

Considering the fine house, filled with equally fine furnishings, and the excellent district in which the family resided, Zoe personally judged the woman more avaricious than genuinely needy. Their standard of living might not equal that enjoyed by Alexis and Sofia themselves, but it was far above the average. Some people were never satisfied.

Treated with scant ceremony herself, she was more than happy to be up and away again. Sofia drew a breath of sheer relief when they were once more in the car.

'I'm glad that is over,' she said frankly. 'I have tried to feel the way I should for Aunt Ariadne, but she makes it very difficult.'

'Does Alexis know her views?' asked Zoe.

'He knows. He took Uncle Lambis into the business because he felt that Father had been too hard in denying him any part in it, but there has never been any gratitude.'

'I'd have thought he would have inherited equal control along with your father,' Zoe commented diffidently, aware that it was none of her affair.

'He gave up his interest in exchange for a cash settlement,' came the reply. 'He regretted it when he saw the success and expansion Father was achieving, and wanted to become involved again, but Father said no.'

Leaving Alexis to fulfil family obligation on his death. It said a lot for him, Zoe reflected, that he still continued to fulfil it, considering the total lack of appreciation.

'The way of the world,' she said. 'I don't blame you for not falling over yourself to keep in regular contact.'

Sofia laughed. 'I would find it difficult to fall over *myself*!'

'A figure of speech.' Zoe was happy to have afforded diversion. 'Do we go home for lunch?'

'I told Artemis that we would, so we must. She would ! : very angry if there was no one to eat the food she will have prepared.'

Artemis did all the cooking in addition to looking after the general running of the household. She was, Zoe reckoned, inexhaustible. Mimosa was her whole life; she scarcely ever left the place. When the time eventually came that she could no longer perform her duties to her satisfaction, she would probably lie down and die.

Arriving back at the villa to find Alexis already home was something of a shock. Zoe had counted on a few more hours in which to prepare herself for confrontation. She couldn't bring herself to meet the dark eyes directly.

'We paid a visit on Aunt Ariadne,' explained Sofia when he asked where they had been. 'Zoe enjoyed it no more than I did myself.'

'Not so surprising,' he said drily. 'However, I'm pleased that you made the effort.' His glance returned to Zoe. 'You look flushed,' he observed.

'It's the weather,' she claimed. 'Is it usually this hot in April?'

'This last year or two it has been. To do with general global warming, I believe.' He paused. 'I'd suggest that you take full advantage of siesta this afternoon, and retire to a darkened room for rest. It will be good for you.'

Almost in the region of an order, Zoe thought, but not a bad idea. At the very least, it would keep her out of his way. She stole a glance at him, unable to penetrate the enigmatic expression. It was difficult to believe now that he had held her so close and so passionately in his arms a few hours ago; that he had said the things he had said to her. Could it all have been a dream, perhaps?

Hardly likely, came the thought. She could still recall the imprint of his lips on hers, the tingling warmth of his hand on her breast. The same sensual stirring was happening right now, induced by the very sight of him.

Lunch was an ordeal. Not least because Alexis himself seemed so utterly indifferent. Whatever his assertions last night, he was of a different mind now, it seemed certain. She should be relieved, not despondent, Zoe told herself. The affair would have brought her nothing but grief. Best now just to forget the whole thing—the way he appeared to have done.

Easier said than done, she found when later she lay in the darkened room as ordained. Her body refused to listen to the dictates of her mind. Alexis had woken a yearning that went beyond lust—that went beyond anything she had ever felt before. She was in love with the man, and there was no getting away from it. Hopelessly, helplessly in love.

She had taken off her outer clothing before she lay down on the bed. Brought to life by the rising temperature, the air-conditioning unit sent a light breeze over her bare skin. Like fingers, she thought, except that Alexis's had been so much more sensitised to her needs and desires, had known just where to linger, where to captivate. To make love with such a man would be an experience out of this world. Only it wasn't going to happen. Not now. The moment was past and gone.

The quiet opening of the door went unnoticed. Eyes closed, mind and body preoccupied, she was unaware of any other presence until the mattress dipped to some added weight.

'I can wait no longer,' said Alexis softly. 'I want you now, *agapi mou*!'

CHAPTER FIVE

RESISTANCE was furthest from Zoe's mind as the strong arms closed about her. She met Alexis's lips with a passion equal to his own, oblivious to everything but the fact that he was here with her, answering her need of him.

He was wearing nothing but a silk robe, which it took him only a moment to shed. The feel of warm, naked flesh was a spur to the emotions already overwhelming her. She said his name, her voice low and tremulous, felt his hand take hers and guide it to him, his lips kissing her eyes, her cheek, teeth nibbling the lobe of her ear.

'You thought to keep me like a puppet on a string,' he murmured thickly. 'Such foolishness! Kiss me. Let your lips tell me what you feel. Such beautiful, tantalising, outspoken lips!'

She was beyond denying him anything. Her body had a will of its own, pressing closer, moving against him in sensual invitation. Inhibition had flown; she was filled with a soaring sense of freedom and elation. She had lived her life for this moment, this man. Wonderful, masterful, totally irresistible Alexis!

His laugh came low and triumphant. Hands skilful, he removed her scanty undergarments and tossed them carelessly aside. She watched him through slitted eyes, loving the look of him: sun-darkened skin stretched taut over bone and muscle. Her skin was pale against his, almost luminous in the dimness of the shaded room.

Every nerve in her body tremored to his caressing exploration, fluttering beneath his stroking, seeking fingers.

He left no single inch of her untouched, smoothing each curve, searching out every crevice, making her gasp and writhe in mindless torment as he took possession of her very soul. His lips followed where his hands had passed, lingeringly, erotically, his tongue a flickering flame that set her alight.

Then he was over her and above her, the potent male weight of him a pressure she couldn't and didn't want to resist. Her body was open and moist, craving the incursion of his flesh.

She arched to meet him as he moved inside her, gently at first, the thrusts penetrating deeper by slow degrees. There was a moment when he seemed to hesitate, followed by a fleeting, soon-forgotten pain as they came wholly and completely together at last. The sensations flooding her were too all-enveloping for any rational thought to find purchase: a pulsing heat that commanded her to move, to thrust in unison with that escalating rhythm, to dig her fingers into the tautly stretched muscles of his back in frenzy as the surge inside her expanded to a point where she could no longer contain it. She cried out as the wave crested, and then again at the incredible hot rush of his release.

In those first moments, lying there with the proud dark head cradled on her breast, Zoe knew no regret, just utter contentment. Nothing she had read or heard had come anywhere close to describing the reality of this total fulfilment. Words could never be enough. Her whole body felt so wonderfully replete. If she wanted anything at all, it was to tell Alexis that she loved him. Because she did. More than she had ever thought it possible to love anyone.

It was only the lift of his head that stopped her from blurting it out. She looked into the dark eyes in silence, unable to read the expression she saw there.

'Why did you allow me to believe you experienced in the ways of love?' he asked harshly. 'This is the first time you ever lay with a man, isn't it?'

Zoe swallowed on the sudden dryness in her throat. 'Was it so obvious?' she whispered. 'Where did I fail you?'

His lips twitched. 'You didn't fail me. Not in the sense you mean. It's a gratification to be the first to possess a woman—to know her the way no other man has known her. You gave me a pleasure more intense than any I've ever known before.'

'Then why,' she asked huskily, 'are you angry?'

'Because you lied to me. Because you led me to believe you available for the taking.' His hands were either side of her head, holding her still so that he could see her face. 'Why?'

He had raised the top half of his body from her, but his hips still pinioned her. She moved a little beneath him, and felt a stirring between her thighs as life and substance began to return to him. Anger was no barrier to renewal, it seemed.

His lips widened unwillingly at the look in her eyes. 'So it happens again. Sometimes the mind has little command of the body. But first you will answer me.'

Zoe sought for words, aware of the forces building again inside her in response to the slowly increasing pressure of his regeneration. Instinctively she adjusted her position, hungry for the feel of him inside her again, moving her body in wanton summons. He groaned low in his throat and responded, not gently this time but with full, fierce thrusts that stirred something deep and primitive in her, carrying her with him to a swift, rushing climax that left them both totally consumed.

It was several minutes before either of them could summon the strength or will to make a move. Minutes during which Zoe found herself drifting close to sleep.

She came awake again with a jerk when Alexis rolled away from her to sit up.

'You leave me no alternative but to remove myself from temptation,' he said gruffly, 'before I lose every ounce of my self-respect. I wouldn't have come to you at all had I known you were still a virgin.'

Zoe forcibly subdued the urge to reach out a hand and stroke the broad back turned to her. 'It had to happen some time,' she murmured.

Alexis turned then to look at her, his jaw tensing as his gaze swept the length of her body. 'With the man who becomes your husband, not just any man!'

'You're not just *any* man.' It was becoming more and more difficult to keep her voice from cracking. 'I fail to see why my being a virgin should make any difference. I'm the same person you wanted last night.'

'No,' he returned, 'you are not. That person existed only in my mind. What did you hope to gain by deceiving me this way?'

'Nothing,' she denied. 'It wasn't intentional. None of this was intentional.' She raised herself on an elbow, mortifyingly aware of her nudity. The fact that Alexis too was devoid of clothing was no comfort. For him, nothing that had happened between them was new. 'I couldn't help myself,' she claimed.

'You found the strength of will to refuse me last night,' he pointed out. 'Why not today?'

'Because my will-power wasn't up to doing it again.'

'Or because you thought to place me under obligation to you, perhaps?'

'That's not true!' She was desperate to deny the accusation. 'I want nothing from you!'

There was no softening in the dark eyes. 'You may already have gained something from me. Unless you prepared in advance for the event?'

She gazed at him blankly for a moment before realisation dawned. A black cloud bore down suddenly on
her head. 'No,' she admitted numbly.

'And I, as you may have noted, was also unprotected.
A foolish omission in this day and age, I admit, but...'
He paused, lifting his shoulders in an expressive shrug.
'Too late for regrets.'

It was all Zoe could do to keep her voice from reflecting the turmoil going on inside her. 'It doesn't have
to happen. And even if it did...' It was her turn to pause,
stomach churning at the look in his eyes.

'And if it did?' he prompted.

She rallied herself to complete the sentence. 'It would
be my problem, not yours.'

He drew in a sharp breath, his jawline tautened to a
degree that made the skin about his mouth look white.
'You believe me the kind of man who would turn his
back on such a responsibility?'

Zoe looked back at him helplessly. 'What's the point
in talking about it at all unless it becomes necessary?
Can't we just forget the whole thing for the time being?'

The strong mouth acquired an ironic line. 'You would
find that easy?'

She would find it impossible, Zoe acknowledged. To
live in the same house as Alexis after this would also be
impossible. Whatever desire he had had for her, it was
surely gone now. That the emotions he had aroused in
her were in no way diminished was her hard luck.

'I think the best thing all round is that I leave,' she
said heavily. 'It wouldn't be too difficult to find some
plausible excuse for Sofia. I could say that my mother
was ill, or something.'

Alexis reached for the robe he had discarded and
pulled it on, standing up to tie the belt about his middle.
'Now isn't the time to make any such decisions. I have
an engagement this evening, so we must wait until to-

morrow to discuss the matter further.' His glance lingered
for a moment on her face, expression remote, before he
turned away abruptly.

Zoe sank back into the pillows as the door closed in
his wake. She felt totally drained of emotion. No matter
what happened, there was no way she could stay here
now.

Christa's arrival some twenty-four hours later was a total
surprise. Alexis had been absent all day, so it was left
to the two girls to greet the newcomer—Zoe with some
reserve.

'I had to come and see how you were getting along,'
confessed the woman, sounding only faintly apologetic.
'I thought I owed it to you to explain in person. You
must have called me a great many unpleasant names
when you discovered that Alexis knew nothing of the
arrangement.'

'One or two,' Zoe agreed, seeing no reason to soft-
pedal. 'It was hardly an ideal situation.'

'But you obviously managed to convince my brother
to allow you to stay on,' Christa pointed out on a note
of satisfaction. 'I look forward to hearing how you
managed it.'

'Sofia helped by begging him to let me stay,' returned
Zoe, wondering what the other was going to say to her
leaving again so soon. She added swiftly, 'I'm still on
trial.'

'Having come this far, he's unlikely to go back on the
arrangement.' Christa shook her head as if still slightly
bemused by the whole affair. 'He didn't sound even re-
motely sympathetic to the cause when he telephoned the
first time.'

'I suppose he was still too angry over the way it had
been done. It wasn't until dinner that he told me he'd
changed his mind about sending me away.'

'All the same, a very rapid alteration. You must have been very convincing.'

Sofia gave a girlish giggle. 'Zoe told Alexis that she objected to his attitude. I don't think anyone had ever said such a thing to him before.'

'I don't imagine they had.' Christa sounded gratified. 'I made the right choice in all respects, it seems.'

Zoe looked at her enquiringly. '*All* respects?'

'It had to be someone capable of standing up to Alexis, in addition to providing the right kind of companionship for Sofia.'

'We spent a whole evening in the Plaka,' put in her sister. 'Zoe persuaded Alexis to accompany us.'

'It didn't take very much persuasion,' disclaimed Zoe hastily.

There was a sudden speculation in the other's regard as she registered Zoe's heightened colour. 'If Alexis allowed himself to be induced at all, it could only be because he wanted to be.'

'He wanted to be with Sofia, of course,' Zoe agreed, and saw Christa's mouth take on a slant reminiscent of her brother's.

'Of course.' There was a pause, a change of tone. 'You'll be staying the full year?'

Zoe made a pretence of correcting the position of her poolside lounger. 'Providing nothing happens to change things.'

Sofia looked at her in sudden perturbation. 'What could happen to take you away?'

'A year is a long time,' Zoe prevaricated. 'You might find you no longer need me.'

'That is not so!' The statement was emphatic. 'You are my dearest friend. I could not bear to lose you!'

Considering the circumstances, she was going to have to bear it, thought Zoe unhappily. Alexis's failure to put in an appearance could only mean that he had, after all, decided that there was nothing more to say on the subject. Which left the ball fairly and squarely in her court.

'It would be wonderful,' continued the younger girl wistfully, 'if you married Alexis. Then we would really be sisters.'

Conscious of Christa's eyes on her, Zoe forced a laugh. 'You already have a sister.'

'Of whom she sees very little,' put in the latter smoothly. 'It's high time Alexis did take a wife, though. Leda Kazantzi meets all his requirements.'

Was that a warning? wondered Zoe, keeping her expression carefully neutral. Did Christa suspect that her feelings for Alexis were more than they should be? And if this Leda was so eminently suitable, why had he not already made the move?

Sofia pulled a face. 'I don't want *her* as a sister. She is far too conceited!'

Christa laughed. 'She has a lot to be conceited about. Not all Greek women have managed to achieve the kind of independence Leda enjoys. She'd make the perfect wife for a man like Alexis.'

'I was under the impression,' said Zoe with control, 'that your brother was a traditionalist?'

'Meaning he'd prefer a home-maker?' Christa shook her head. 'He'd be bored out of his mind with a woman like that. I've come to know my brother very well in these past years since we became a family again. He needs a wife who can meet him on every level. Leda is not only beautiful, but highly intelligent too. She speaks both French and English fluently, and has travelled over much of the world already, although she's still only in her mid-twenties.'

'You obviously know her very well,' murmured Zoe, stifling the pangs.

'She stays with us from time to time when she visits England. Her family home is right here in Athens. The Kazantzis are very influential.'

And wealthy, Zoe surmised. That went without saying. A Westernised outlook too, it appeared, if a daughter of the house was allowed such latitude. The fact that Sofia didn't like the woman was something of a comfort. Not that it made any difference whatsoever to her own position. Handling her departure without giving herself away was going to call for all her ingenuity.

Christa changed the subject after that. When not putting matters into proper perspective, she displayed the same friendly cordiality that Zoe remembered from her interviews.

'It's going to be quite a shock for Al... Kyrios Theodorou to find you here when he gets back,' she remarked, biting back the familiarity.

Christa shrugged good-humouredly. 'Alexis is well accustomed to *my* independence. I may even stay over Easter and get my husband to join me. It's time he had a break.'

'We're sailing down to the islands after next weekend,' said Sofia. 'Why do you and David not come too?'

'It's a temptation,' Christa admitted. Her gaze flicked to Zoe. 'You'll be going with them?'

'Of course Zoe is coming,' declared her sister. 'As if we would leave her behind!'

'I feel extremely privileged,' acknowledged Zoe, aware that she must keep up the pretence. 'I never expected such good fortune.'

'You could hardly have anticipated a life of deprivation,' came the dry response. 'You were, I'm sure, well aware of the family circumstances.'

'I naturally accepted the probability that I'd be living a very comfortable life out here, yes. Beyond that, I didn't give it a great deal of thought. I'm very lucky to have the opportunity—and very grateful to you, *kyria*, for providing it. Even though,' she added with purpose, 'you did drop me in at the deep end!'

The other allowed herself to smile. 'But not without first making sure you could swim.'

'Zoe is an excellent swimmer,' claimed Sofia, taking the remark at face value. 'She's teaching me the butterfly stroke. Would you like to see?'

'Very much.' The older, but no less lovely face had softened to indulgence. 'After which I must go and change into something a little more comfortable. I feel very travel-weary.'

She looked bandbox-fresh, thought Zoe, taking in the classic lines of Christa's pale grey linen dress, the smooth styling of the luxuriant black hair, and immaculate makeup. Whether David Townsend had been rich nineteen years ago, she had no way of knowing, but he certainly wasn't struggling now. Both his London home and his wife were proof of that.

Sofia put up a creditable performance, and was duly applauded. She was acquiring a whole new confidence, Zoe reflected, for which she herself was entitled to take some credit. She was going to miss the girl so much. And for what? A few minutes of dubious pleasure with a man who didn't even care for her.

Hardly dubious, came the immediate and honest rider. Alexis's lovemaking left nothing to be desired; her body tremored to the very memory of it. If there was fault to be found, it was her own for failing to acknowledge her lack of experience. None of this would have happened, had he known she was still a virgin.

There was still no sign of him when she went to her room around seven that evening on the pretext of having some letters to write before dinner. She had to be the cause of his absence, thought Zoe hollowly. Perhaps he was even hoping that she would have gone when he did

get back. If there had been any way short of simply
walking out, she might have obliged him, too. It was
only the thought of Sofia's reaction that kept her here.

She considered crying off dinner that evening on the
grounds of having developed a bad headache, but dis-
missed the idea as too self-indulgent. She had to carry
on as normal until she had worked out just how she was
going to arrange the phoney summons home. Having
telephoned only yesterday, she could hardly use family
illness as an excuse. Her best bet might be to get one of
her friends back home to telephone through with news
of an accident. Not a fatal one, of course, but serious
enough to necessitate her immediate return.

And what did she tell the friend she asked to perform
the favour? came the depressing question. There were
pitfalls whichever way she looked. She had at the most
a couple of days to come up with something. That was
going to be about the limit of her endurance.

Finding the master of the house alone in the *saloni*
when she eventually went down was a shock to her whole
system because she had convinced herself that he
wouldn't be here for dinner either. It was too late to
retreat, she acknowledged, as he turned from the lac-
quered cabinet, where he had been pouring a drink, to
look across at her with an unfathomable expression.

'You would like an ouzo too?' he asked.

Zoe steeled herself to meet the dark eyes full-on. 'I'd
rather have a gin and lime, please.'

'As you prefer.' He put ice into a glass, poured the
requested mix, and brought both glasses across to where
she had taken a seat.

Zoe took the glass from him, reminded all too vividly
of the last time—was it really only two nights ago?—
that they had drunk together in this same room. She was
even occupying the same seat, although not inten-
tionally. At least, she didn't think so.

Scooped wide enough at the neckline to reveal the delicate boning of her shoulders, the turquoise print dress she had chosen at random from her wardrobe made her feel vulnerable under his gaze. She had taken her hair back from her face in order to tame the riotous curls a little, which didn't help either. This close, she couldn't bring herself to look at him directly, but murmured her thanks with eyes raised no further than the middle button of his cream silk shirt.

'There are matters we have to discuss,' he said on a note of determination. 'You will——'

'So here you are at last!' Superb in slim-skirted white silk jersey, Christa came sweeping into the room. Her glance skipped lightly over Zoe's face before coming back to her brother's. 'We thought you'd decided to leave home!'

'I had business to take care of,' he returned. 'Artemis told me of your arrival. Why didn't you let me know you were coming?'

'It was a spur-of-the-moment decision to accompany Leda.' The eyes so like his own were bland. 'You knew she'd been with us this last week?'

'I knew she was in England,' he said. 'Is she well?'

'Wonderfully so! She sends her regards, and asked that you call her.'

Sofia's arrival checked whatever reply he might have been about to make, although his expression, Zoe judged, had not exactly been one of pleasure. A dislike of having messages relayed through his sister, perhaps? If Leda Kazantzi had been out of the country until this afternoon, she had obviously not been the one to claim his attentions the previous evening—for all the good that knowledge did her. He might have a dozen would-be brides dangling on strings until he made up his mind. The only thing certain was that *she* wasn't one of them.

He was his usual urbane self over dinner. Zoe's request that they conduct conversation in their own language was largely ignored. All three were bilingual, while her grasp of Greek was still in its infancy, so it made sense, she supposed, if she wasn't to be left sitting here in comparative silence. All the same, she felt intrusive in a way she hadn't done before this.

There was still room available, Alexis confirmed when Sofia repeated her suggestion that Christa and David join the cruise.

'It's to be just a few close friends, no business associates,' he added. 'I intend to relax.'

'And not before time.' Christa paused before adding casually, and still in English, 'Shall you be inviting Leda? It would be a fine opportunity for the two of you to be together.'

The firm mouth acquired a thinner line. He answered in the same language. 'That isn't the purpose. I've asked you before to stay out of my affairs, Christa. I'll choose for myself when the time comes.'

'Of course you will.' She was totally unabashed. 'Just don't leave it too long.'

'At midnight tomorrow we enter Holy Week,' said Sofia to Zoe before her brother could give vent to the anger sparking in his eyes. 'Some of the more devout will have fasted for the whole of Lent, but many, as we do ourselves, only pay tribute in the final days. You won't be expected to go without meat yourself, of course.'

Considering that she didn't intend being here for the most of it, it scarcely mattered, Zoe reflected. She said levelly, 'I'd prefer to follow the custom.'

His anger with his sister apparently shelved for the moment, Alexis looked across at her with a veiled expression. 'Now might be the time to mention that on Good Friday we observe a day of total fast,' he said. 'You wish to follow that custom also?'

An intimation that he'd prefer her to be gone before then? Zoe wondered hollowly. Pride kept her voice rock-steady. 'Why not? I'm a Christian too.'

The brief inclination of his head could have meant anything. Zoe avoided glancing in Christa's direction, suspecting that the other might well have misinterpreted her apparent willingness to take part in the Easter rites. The woman was already aware that her feelings for Alexis went rather deeper than those expected of a mere employee. It was to be hoped that she never guessed just how far those feelings had led her.

Her suspicions were confirmed later when Christa suggested that the two of them take a stroll in the gardens before retiring for the night. Alexis looked a little surprised at the request, but made no comment. They left him finishing off his brandy in the *saloni* with Sofia for company.

The older woman waited several moments before broaching the subject that Zoe already knew was coming. Her tone was pleasant enough, but left little doubt of her intention.

'I thought it best to warn you against allowing yourself to become too enamoured of my brother,' she said. 'He's a very attractive man, I know, but it's highly unlikely that he'd consider you in any other light than that of an employee.'

'What makes you so sure I am enamoured, as you put it?' asked Zoe with control, determined to allow herself to show neither anger nor resentment. 'You've only been here a few hours.'

'Long enough to observe the way you react even to the mention of his name.' She paused, as if searching for the right words. 'I only want to save you pain, Zoe. Alexis might have shown you consideration, even indulgence, for Sofia's sake, but it means nothing more, I can assure you. If he responds to you as a man—and

I can see for myself that he does—then it's only in the way that any male might respond to a pretty face and figure, and still means nothing. However, he *is* a man, and given encouragement . . .'

Zoe's voice sounded heavy in her ears. 'You're telling me he might see fit to indulge himself if the opportunity presented itself? Leaving aside my own code of ethics, it doesn't say very much for your brother's either.'

Christa gave a faint smile. 'If there's one thing I've learned it's that the majority of men share the same attitude towards sexual liaisons.'

'You include your own husband in that assessment?'

'Certainly. David is no more immune from temptation than any other.'

'That's a very cynical attitude.'

'I prefer to call it a realistic one. You're an extremely attractive young woman, and you make no secret of your feelings towards Alexis. Why should he not take advantage?'

The intimation that she wore her heart on her sleeve was dismaying. Zoe was hard put to retain any sense of proportion. 'In the circumstances,' she said, 'wouldn't it have been prudent to have hired a companion who was unlikely to provide any temptation at all?'

'There were several applicants who might have filled that role,' Christa admitted, 'but they weren't suitable in other respects. I chose you for the position because of all those I interviewed you appeared to be the most level-headed and responsible. You've already endeared yourself to Sofia, and I'm fairly sure that your feelings for her are genuine too. All I ask is that you remember the reason you're here, and that you can just as easily be removed.'

'Even at the cost of upsetting Sofia just as she's beginning to enjoy our relationship?'

Christa came to an abrupt halt, face suddenly hardened. 'She would soon forget you.'

Zoe was already regretting the ill-considered words. Sofia had no part in this. 'I'm sorry,' she said levelly. 'That was wrong of me.'

'Yes, it was.' Christa waited a moment, as though expecting more, then sighed and continued walking along the shadowed pathway. 'I don't mean to sound harsh, but you must realise for yourself that nothing could come of any alliance between you and Alexis.'

It was useless to keep on denying any emotional involvement, Zoe conceded with resignation. Christa was too astute. 'I do realise it,' she said. 'And you have nothing to be concerned about. I would no more aspire to interest a man such as Kyrios Theodorou than he would lower himself to take interest in me!'

'You called him Alexis at dinner,' came the smooth retort. 'You wouldn't have done that if he hadn't given you permission. He isn't a man to encourage familiarity as a matter of course, which means that he regards you in a more intimate light than others of the staff. I think we can take his interest for granted. Just be sure it goes no further than that.'

They had reached the little temple. Christa indicated that they should return the way they had come, apparently satisfied that she had said all that needed to be said. Zoe trailed a little to the rear, inwardly seething. Everything else aside, who was this woman to lay down the law with regard to rules of behaviour? She might have instigated the job, but Alexis had taken over the role of employer.

Alexis. It all came back to Alexis. A definite interest, Christa had noted, but she was misinterpreting that too. His only interest now must lie in extricating himself from a situation which was, to say the least, undesirable.

They found him alone in the *saloni*. Sofia, he said, had gone to bed. He eyed the two of them with a thoughtfully narrowed gaze.

'An enjoyable stroll?' he asked.

'Extremely,' replied his sister lightly. 'I'm feeling quite weary myself. You won't mind if I follow Sofia's example and leave you?'

'Not at all,' he said. 'We'll have time enough to-morrow to talk together.'

'I'll say goodnight too,' said Zoe expressionlessly.

'In a moment.' It was almost a command. 'There's something I wish to discuss with you.'

About to start for the door, Christa hesitated, glancing at her brother in obvious uncertainty, then back to Zoe herself with an all too easily read message in her eyes. Zoe returned the look without a flicker. What was she supposed to do?

Unable to turn back from her stated intention without appearing to be over-inquisitive, the other woman continued on her way. Alexis indicated that Zoe should take a seat, waiting until his sister had closed the door before making any attempt to open the conversation. She fixed her eyes on the brown column of his throat, willing herself to ignore the churning in her stomach. There was only one thing he could want to say to her, and that was to tell her she was to go.

'What did Christa tell you out there?' he asked without preamble, startling her into meeting the dark gaze full-on.

'I'm not sure what you mean,' she said. 'We just walked.'

'I don't believe you. Your face, when you came back just now, gave you away. I want to know what it was she said to you.'

'Why don't you ask her?' she prevaricated.

There was no relenting of expression. 'I'm asking *you*. And I mean to have an answer!'

Anger came to her rescue. As if she hadn't already gone through enough! 'And no one refuses Alexis Theodorou anything, of course!' she said bitingly. 'Well, this is one time you're not getting your own way. If you want to know what we talked about, then you ask your sister to tell you herself!'

He was on his feet before she had finished speaking, crossing the space between them in a couple of strides to drag her forcibly into his arms. His mouth was savage on hers, trapping her protests in her throat. Only when she stopped struggling against him did he let up the pressure, holding her a little away from him to look into her eyes with a blaze in his own.

'Tell me!'

Shaken to the core, Zoe could hardly get the words out. 'She warned me against letting myself become involved with you, if you must know. A pity she didn't arrive earlier. She might have saved us both a lot of trouble.'

'What happened between the two of us would have done so regardless at some time,' came the hard reply. 'What made Christa suspect that there might be an interest on your part if you didn't tell her so yourself?'

'She guessed. I'm obviously not very good at concealing my feelings.'

His gaze narrowed. 'You're telling me your emotions are involved?'

'Don't be ridiculous!' Zoe was too intent on salvaging what little pride she had left to care what she said. 'I was bowled over by lust, that's all!'

The hands still holding her upper arms tautened painfully. 'Do not,' he gritted, 'speak to me in that manner! Many things I may be, but I won't have a woman tell me I'm ridiculous!'

'I'm sorry.' The apology was stiff but sincere. 'It wasn't meant the way it sounded.'

'Then why use the word at all?' The anger was still running high. He put her from him abruptly, turning away to reclaim the glass he had set down with almost enough force to shatter so few moments before. 'You'd better be seated again,' he said. 'Whether you like it or not, there are things we have to talk about.'

Zoe obeyed for the simple reason that her legs were threatening to let her down anyway. She felt so utterly wretched about this whole affair. That Alexis still found her physically desirable had been only too obvious when he had held her so tightly against him a moment or two ago. He had said it himself: the mind could not always control the body. She wanted him, too, more than she dared allow herself to acknowledge. Except that, for her, wanting was an integral part of loving, and that was where the difference lay.

'I'm prepared to go as soon as I can find a reasonable excuse for Sofia,' she said, low-toned. 'The last thing I'd want is for her to know the truth. I imagine you feel that way too.'

Alexis was in full command of himself again, face registering nothing of his thoughts. 'Naturally. She'll know only what she must know.' The pause was brief, his tone, when he spoke again, uncompromising. 'The marriage will take place when we return from the cruise.'

CHAPTER SIX

How long she just sat there in stunned silence, Zoe couldn't have said. Her mind was spinning. A bare week ago she hadn't even met this man!

A bare week ago she hadn't known what love was either, came the thought—in any context. One-sided still so far as Alexis was concerned, for certain. He was doing this from some misguided sense of obligation.

'It's more than generous of you,' she got out at last, 'but quite unnecessary to go that far. You owe me nothing.'

The dark eyes were lit by inner turbulence. 'And the child you may even now be carrying? You consider that nothing?'

'It doesn't have to be that way,' she said with mentally crossed fingers. 'The odds are that I'm not.'

'The odds,' he returned, 'have little bearing. What kind of a man would I be if I waited to see the outcome of my action before offering recompense?'

'I don't want recompense!' She was desperate to convince him. 'I know you consider love unessential in marriage, but I don't. And there are other factors too. I'm not even of your world, Alexis. How could you, in your position, marry a nobody from England?'

He regarded her in silence for a lengthy moment. 'Does your father consider himself a nobody too?' he asked.

She flushed. 'No, of course not. I didn't mean it like that.'

'Then what did you mean?'

She spread her hands in a helpless gesture. 'You need a wife from the same environment. Someone accustomed to your ways. I can barely speak the language.'

'Time and practice will take care of that. As our ways can also be learned. They aren't so very different from your own.'

'Yes, they are. Your whole concept of marriage is different. You regard wives as possessions, like any other. Where I come from marriage is a partnership, with both participants holding equal rights.'

'Could that, perhaps, be why the incidence of divorce is so much greater in your country?' He made an impatient movement. 'This is foolish talk!'

'Which still leaves love,' Zoe continued with determination. 'I could never marry anyone without that.'

Some flicker of an unreadable expression crossed the strong features. 'You'd even deny your child a name for lack of it?'

Which brought them right back to square one, Zoe acknowledged. 'There's a good chance that it won't happen,' she repeated. 'Why jump into something we'll both of us regret if it turned out to be unnecessary after all?'

Alexis continued to regard her with the same narrowed intensity. 'You're saying you'll accept only if you prove to be pregnant?'

Was that what she was saying? Zoe wasn't sure any longer. Marriage hadn't entered her head when she had welcomed him into her bed; she had looked no further than the quenching of the thirst he had aroused. Last night and today her thoughts had been only of escape from a situation with which she could no longer cope. How could she now suddenly start contemplating a future with Alexis as a husband?

'I need to get away,' she said huskily. 'I can't think straight!'

'No.' The tone was unequivocal. 'I refuse to allow it!'

She looked at him with a set expression, concealing her emotions behind a resolute façade. 'You can't stop me from leaving.'

'I can, and will,' he stated, 'if I must.'

'How? By locking me up? You'd have difficulty explaining *that* away to Sofia!'

'She would have to know the truth,' he agreed. 'She'd be rightly shocked that her newest and dearest friend should not only have shared a bed with a man before marriage, and so soon after meeting, but refuses to allow him to right the wrong he has done her.'

Zoe swallowed on the hard little lump in her throat. Sofia would not just be shocked, she would be devastated. Bad enough for her to realise that Zoe herself was far from the person she had believed her to be, but worse to have her beloved brother revealed as seducer.

'I don't believe you'd do that to her,' she said haltingly.

There was no change in the hard, incisive line of his mouth. 'The choice lies with you.' He waited a moment for her response, accepting her silence as capitulation. 'How long before you know your condition?'

Her colour deepened. 'A little over a week.'

'By which time we'll all be aboard the *Hestia*.' The pause was brief. 'So we wait.'

A reprieve of sorts, she thought hollowly. Many might call her a fool for not leaping at the chance he had offered her, but how long could a marriage based on such shaky foundations last? If she did prove to be pregnant, she was going to have to find some way of persuading him to put aside his sense of duty, because the same would apply. In the meantime, it was going to be necessary to act as if nothing at all had happened, for Sofia's sake.

She found herself on her feet without really knowing how she had got there. 'If that's all,' she said tonelessly, 'I'll say goodnight.'

Alexis made no attempt to stop her as she moved to the door. He was still standing in the same position when she glanced back just before closing it on him, his face taut and alien. He had made the supreme gesture, and had it thrown back at him. His pride wouldn't make for easy acceptance.

It was a harrowing week altogether. Never very much good at acting, Zoe found it just about impossible to behave naturally when Alexis was around. Sofia appeared to notice nothing, but it was obvious that Christa wasn't wholly deceived, although the woman made no actual comment.

Fasting midnight to midnight on Good Friday was no great hardship because she didn't feel much like eating anyway. Church bells tolled funeral knells, signifying a sorrow that was two thousand years old yet no less deeply felt. Zoe found herself entering into the spirit of the occasion and exercising the same restraint on laughter and idle conversation. She and her parents had always attended church services at Easter in particular, but she had never before known this same sense of involvement.

It was Alexis's suggestion that they all drive into Athens to watch the principal funeral procession that began and ended in the cathedral. Zoe had the feeling that the gesture was for her benefit as the rest of them must have seen the spectacle many times before, but she was grateful for the thought.

They had seats on a balcony of the Grande Bretagne Hotel, overlooking Syntagma Square, and the crowds gathered in readiness. Perfumed smoke from the smouldering braziers set around the square formed a misty curtain through which the thousands of lighted candles flickered and glowed like fireflies.

Led by the silver-helmeted National Guard, the cortège came into view. In their wake a brass band played the funeral march from Beethoven's *Eroica* Symphony, while behind, in slow cadence, marched troops of boy and girl Scouts, more guardsmen, a contingent of nurses. The melancholy strains of Chopin's *Marche Funebre*, played by yet another brass band, heralded ranks of uniformed military personnel, these in turn followed by schoolboys wearing lilac gowns and holding torches aloft to reveal the bare-headed priest in their wake who carried an empty wooden cross.

Nothing she had ever experienced at this time before, thought Zoe, could compare with what she felt right now. It was as if two thousand years had vanished in the smoke. There was a total hush in the square, and everyone knelt as the flower-decked and canopied bier of Christ passed by, borne by white-robed priests.

Alexis touched her shoulder. 'Do you wish to join the procession back to the cathedral?' he asked softly.

'Yes, please,' she said, blinking through the tears which had formed involuntarily in her eyes. 'I'm sorry for being so emotional. I never expected it to be like this.'

It was too dark to see the expression in his eyes, but his mouth looked relaxed. 'You're not the first to find the ceremony moving,' he acknowledged. 'At midnight tomorrow the whole city will rejoice, and life will return to normal.'

For most, perhaps, she reflected as she moved to accompany him to where Sofia and Christa were waiting. For her, life might never be normal again.

Alexis made sure that the four of them stayed close together as they joined the thousands following the bier through the streets. There was little pushing or shoving, just a general flow. By some miracle, they even managed to get inside the cathedral to see the Archbishop of Athens lead the bier into the inner sanctum, where he exchanged his golden crown for an everyday black hat before emerging again to bless the faithful, and offer the solace of Resurrection in the words of St Paul to the Corinthians.

Zoe related the psalm in English to herself as he spoke: 'I will unfold the mystery: we shall not all die, but we shall all be changed in a flash, in the twinkling of an eye, at the last trumpet-call ... And when our mortality has been clothed with immortality, then the saying of Scripture will come true: "Death is swallowed up; victory is won!" "O Death, where is your victory? O Death, where is your sting?"'

Midnight brought an end to the day's devotions, and, for the Theodorou party, a return to Politia. There was little conversation in the car. Seated in the rear with Sofia, Zoe closed her eyes and pretended to be asleep while she tried for the umpteenth time to find some way round her situation. The only realistic solution was to cut and run before they embarked on this cruise, and take her chances with the rest. The only thing stopping her from doing just that was the thought of Sofia's disillusionment.

Or was that just an excuse? she asked herself hardily. Was it that she really wanted to stay? Even perhaps wanted her pregnancy confirmed so that she had reason to accept Alexis's offer? She couldn't be sure even of her own mind any more.

There was no attempt on his part to delay her departure tonight. Christa herself seemed subdued as she said goodnight, while Sofia was too weary to be aware of anything but the need for sleep. Lying awake as the hours went by, Zoe wondered if she was ever going to know a wholly peaceful night again.

Arriving on the Saturday afternoon, David Townsend made no secret of the fact that he had deliberately missed out on the fasting. He was a well-built man in his early forties, still displaying the fair good looks that had captured Christa's heart so many years ago. He appeared to get along well enough with Alexis, while Sofia obviously held him in great esteem.

Whether Christa had said anything to him in private about her, Zoe had no way of knowing for sure, although his attitude seemed to suggest it. Several times during dinner she was aware of him watching her—particularly when Alexis happened to address some remark to her. Not exactly a censorious regard, she was bound to admit, but disconcerting all the same.

At eleven o'clock, and once again, she felt, for her benefit more than their own, the whole party headed for Athens again, this time to a vantage-point in sight of Mount Lycabettus.

The chapel of St George at its summit was far too small to accommodate a proper congregation, but as the hour drew near thousands of Athenians formed a shoulder-to-shoulder chain that wound like a serpent down the fir-clad hillside. Just before midnight, the church was plunged into total darkness to symbolise the blackness of the grave, then exactly on the minute came the cry of, '*Christos anesti! Christos anesti!*' and, starting from the top of the hill, candles were lit one from another, passing downwards until the whole crowded summit was aglow.

Fireworks soaring into the sky signalled a sudden and startling change in the mood of the packed throngs below as they exploded into joyous celebration. Candle-light framed rhapsodic faces in golden warmth, the flickering flames threatening hair and clothing alike as the masses milled and surged.

Zoe found herself caught up and swirled away from the others, greeted from all sides with the universal, *'Christos anesti!'* She had practised the proper reply to a point where it tripped from her lips automatically. *'Alithos anesti o Kyrios!'*—the king is risen indeed—drawing smiles and warm embraces from those about her. Extricating herself at length from the main flow, she was taken aback to find Paul Kenyon almost at her side.

'Fantastic, isn't it?' he shouted above the general clamour of church bells, gun salutes and hooting sirens from the ships anchored off Piraeus. 'Are you alone?'

Zoe shook her head and indicated the way she had come. 'The others are back there somewhere. We got separated.'

'Sofia too?' he asked with scarcely concealed eagerness.

'And her brother.' She watched the enthusiasm fade a little. 'Along with her sister and brother-in-law. I'd better try and make my way back. They'll be looking for me.'

'You were going to ring me,' he reminded her. 'I've made a few friends since I saw you. It would be nice if we could all get together some time soon.'

Including Sofia, Zoe surmised. The latter had made no reference to Paul during the past week, which led to the premise that the interest on her part had been short-lived. Excuses for not keeping her promise to contact him could only sound false, she decided. Best to be direct about it.

'I'm afraid we shan't be coming into Athens at all for some time,' she said. 'We'll be on a cruise from Monday.'

'Lucky you!' His voice held a note of wry acceptance. 'Seems as if you found a job in a million!'

Her smile was over-bright. 'You could say that. Anyway, good luck with yours.'

'Thanks.' He moved up alongside when she turned to start threading her way back along the still thronged street. 'I have to go this way too.' His arm came about her waist as she stumbled over a kerb-stone. 'Steady there! If you go down in this lot you'll never get up again!'

He left the arm where it was, guiding her through the crowds. Zoe was relieved to see Alexis coming towards them, although, from the expression which crossed his face as he spotted the two of them, that sentiment played but a minor part in his own responses.

'I got carried away,' she said unnecessarily when he reached them. 'You remember Paul Kenyon?'

'I remember.' The dark eyes reflected the glitter all about him. 'A rare coincidence that the two of you should meet up again amid all this.'

'Isn't it just?' agreed Paul. 'I was with some other people too, but it's just about impossible to stay together with all this going on.' He gave Zoe a final wry glance, obviously recognising his cue to depart. 'Hope you enjoy your cruise. Perhaps we could get together again after you get back?'

'That,' said Alexis tautly, before she could reply, 'will not be possible.' His hand came about her upper arm in a grasp hard enough to bruise. 'Come.'

Zoe allowed herself to be drawn away because this was hardly the time for angry protests. Alexis had no understanding of the word 'casual' when applied to male-female relationships—and especially now when their own relationship hung in such uneasy balance. All the same, he had no right to treat her like some wayward teenager either!

'You're hurting me,' she said, loud enough for him to hear above the general clamour. 'Alexis!'

He turned without speaking and pulled her into the shelter of a doorway, lifting her up on her toes to kiss her with a passion that found an echo in both body and heart. She was unable to say anything at all for a moment or two when he finally put her from him again.

'You belong to *me*!' he gritted. 'No other man will know you!'

'Paul is just an acquaintance,' she protested. 'He means nothing to me. As a matter-of-fact, he's more interested in Sofia than in me.' Seeing his face darken still further, she made haste to add, 'Not that she's the least bit interested in him.'

'I would hope not. It's enough——' He broke off, dismissing what he had been about to say with an abrupt movement of his head. 'We must go and find the others.'

Enough that he himself was entangled with a non-Greek, Zoe surmised grimly. His claim that she belonged to him was no more than simple masculine possessiveness; his self-esteem alone wouldn't allow him to consider the prospect of being succeeded by others. She was in love with a man whose feelings for her went no deeper than that, and she had to accept it. She could only hope that circumstances would relieve him of any further commitment.

They found the other three waiting where Alexis had left them. Christa gave them both what Zoe could only term an old-fashioned look, but made no comment other than to express relief that the missing member had been found so quickly.

It was only when they came under the light of a lamp on reaching the car that Zoe saw the faint smear of pale pink lipstick at the corner of Alexis's mouth, and realised why Christa had looked the way she did. So now she knew—or, at least, some of it. She would not, Zoe was sure, be content to leave it there.

Sunday was a restful day for them all. Zoe did some packing for the boat in the afternoon, while Sofia lounged in a chair, offering advice on what she might need. Artemis would do her packing later, she said. She would have done Zoe's too, had the latter only asked.

'I just can't accustom myself to being waited on,' Zoe acknowledged. 'It's different for you. You grew up to it.'

'Do you think me lazy?' asked the younger girl with a trace of anxiety. 'Should I begin to make more of an effort in my daily life?'

Zoe laughed and shook her head. 'You're fine as you are. Anyway, Artemis would throw a fit if you started making your own bed, et cetera.'

'If you mean she'd be angry, you're right,' Sofia agreed. 'It wouldn't be a kindness to make her so.'

This time Zoe kept a straight face. 'No, it wouldn't.'

Sofia's English was becoming progressively less structured as the days went by, she noted, although she still retained the same attractive accent, of course. Even after nineteen years in England, Christa hadn't entirely lost it either. The intonation in Alexis's voice was a lure in itself—especially when he was in an ardent mood. If only...

She made an effort of her own to shake off the depression threatening to overtake her. What would be, would be.

Christa had requested that English tea be served on the terrace at five for those who wanted it. She had even brought a supply of her favourite blend with her. Emerging from the house alongside Sofia, Zoe scarcely needed the other's murmur of dismay to tell her the identity of the woman talking so animatedly with Alexis.

Leda Kazantzi was perhaps a year or two older than Zoe was, and possessed the kind of looks generally found on magazine covers. Her luxuriant black hair had been styled by an expert to frame her face within its smooth curve, making Zoe doubly conscious of her own unruly mop. Eyes of a startling topaz revealed little friendliness when introductions were performed.

'You must,' she said coolly, 'think yourself very fortunate to have found such a position. It came as a great surprise to learn that Alexis had allowed it.' The last with a smile in his direction. 'Not that I knew what Christa was planning to do, of course.'

If she had she would have told him, Zoe surmised. It was impossible to guess what he might be thinking or feeling at this moment; his expression gave nothing away. Whether Leda had been invited or simply turned up was also uncertain, although she doubted the latter. It was possible, she supposed, that Christa had taken matters into her own hands again, reminding her brother where his best interests lay.

She made her excuses as soon as she reasonably could, and left them to it. Sofia found her at the little temple some time later.

'I have looked everywhere for you,' she said. 'Why did you go so quickly?'

'I felt intrusive,' Zoe confessed.

'Then you should not. You're one of our family now.' Sofia sat down at her side, studying her with some concern. 'Are you no longer happy here, Zoe? Has something happened to change the way you feel?'

'Nothing at all,' Zoe assured her quickly—perhaps too quickly, for the other looked unconvinced. 'It just takes a little getting used to.'

'You've been here almost three whole weeks. Why should it be now that you begin to feel intrusive?' Sofia hesitated, her diffidence returning full force. 'Is it because of Leda?'

Zoe effected a smile and a light shrug. 'She didn't very much like my being there.'

'It is no concern of hers to approve or disapprove!' came the indignant reply. 'You should pay her no heed!

Anyway,' she quietened again to add, 'she won't be accompanying us tomorrow, in spite of all Christa's efforts to persuade Alexis into inviting her. She fails to recognise his unwillingness to be pressured.' There was another pause, another change of tone. 'Do you like Alexis, Zoe?'

'Of course,' she said brightly. 'He's been very generous in allowing me to stay, especially after the things I said to him that first day.'

'I meant, do you find him attractive?'

'He's a very attractive man,' she got out. 'Talking of which, I bumped quite literally into Paul Kenyon during the mêlée last night. He was asking after you.'

For a brief moment Sofia looked blank, then her brow cleared. 'Oh, the one we met in the Agora? I had quite forgotten about him.'

So much for Paul, thought Zoe drily. She made a move to stand up before Sofia could return to the previous topic. 'It's clouded over. I think we might be in for some rain. Shall we get back to the house before it does?'

Aware of the prevarication or not, the other made no protest. Zoe had the feeling that she had already discovered all she needed to know.

After two late nights—or early mornings—no one seemed all that eager to extend this one beyond reasonable limits. They were due to leave for Piraeus at eight o'clock in order to be on board the *Hestia* before the other two couples arrived. The yacht had two staterooms and a further four double cabins, in addition to the saloons and crew's quarters, Zoe had learned from Sofia. No poor man's plaything, for sure.

Up and about again at six, she found that the threatened rain had come and gone in the night, leaving the air freshened and the garden bursting with colour. The early morning sunlight had a brilliant, crystalline quality that made her regret not having brought her camera downstairs with her. Turning back to go and fetch it, she walked straight into Alexis, just emerging from the *saloni*.

The pale blue jeans and white T-shirt he was wearing emphasised his breadth of shoulder and narrowness of hip in a way that quickened Zoe's pulses even more than the physical impact had done. She felt suddenly over-dressed in her neat shirtwaister.

'It will be a casual affair, this cruise of ours,' he said, as if catching her thought. 'We only take trouble in the evening. Jeans or shorts and swimwear will be all you need during the day.'

He made no attempt to move out of her way, registering her discomposure with an ironic smile. 'Don't look so concerned. I'm well aware of the need for discretion. Once on board the *Hestia*, you must relax and enjoy yourself. There's nothing to be gained from anticipating a problem which may not even arise.'

Was he trying to reassure her or himself? Zoe wondered wryly. He could even be right, but she was incapable of pushing the whole thing to the back of her mind that way. The more she saw of him, the worse it was going to be.

'I'll do my best,' she said, conquering the urge to tell him that she would prefer not to go on the cruise at all. Even without Sofia to consider, he was hardly going to agree to her staying here at the villa.

Not that she would be doing, anyway, she acknowledged. She would be on the first available flight home, regardless of the consequences.

Artemis came out with coffee and *koulouria* for them both. She would have been up and about for hours already, Zoe knew, but she never showed any sign of fatigue. Sofia had said that she would take advantage of their absence over the coming two or three weeks to have the whole villa spring-cleaned. She gave Zoe a look of approval on being thanked for the coffee.

'Artemis smiles on very few,' remarked Alexis after the old woman had departed.

'You mean foreigners?' Zoe asked.

'I mean anyone.' He added levelly, 'She'd be enraptured to have a child to look after again.'

Zoe managed to keep her voice reasonably steady. 'Even one conceived outside marriage?'

'Providing the wrong had been righted, she would accept it, yes. She's waited many years for such an event.'

'In the hope, surely, that you'd marry a suitable Greek girl. Leda Kazantzi, for instance.'

Alexis's face darkened. 'Leda has no part in this.'

'But you had considered marrying her?' she insisted, possessed of a sudden and overpowering need to know.

'The matter is not for discussion,' he stated flatly. 'My concern now is only with you. Should you prove to be carrying my child, it will be necessary to marry both quickly and quietly.'

'Wouldn't that simply emphasise the reason?'

'You'd prefer to wait until you emphasised it some other way?' he asked drily. 'Your parents would have to be informed, of course.' He paused. 'The time must be close by now when you'll have some indication of your condition?'

A bit late to start being coy about such matters, Zoe conceded, trying to formulate the same down-to-earth approach. 'Within a couple of days, hopefully.' She was almost relieved to see Christa and David emerging from the house, although the former's expression as she viewed the two of them was far from encouraging.

'And I thought *we* were early!' she remarked.

Clad as comfortably and casually as Alexis himself, she prompted Zoe to get to her feet. 'I'm going up to change into something more suitable before my suitcase is brought down,' she said.

She met Sofia on the way, pausing only long enough to exchange a determinedly cheerful greeting. Once in her room, she got out of the pink and white dress and extracted a pair of pale blue denim jeans from her suitcase, along with a sleeveless cotton top in black. It was the first time she had worn either item here.

Studying her reflection in the cheval mirror, she found herself smoothing a questing hand over her flat stomach, and gave a wry little smile. There couldn't possibly be any sign as yet.

With sandals exchanged for lightweight trainers, she swiftly straightened out her suitcase and closed it again, ready for Yannis to take down along with the others. He would be following with the luggage in another car, taking one of the other men with him to drive the Mercedes back from the port at Zea, where the yacht was moored. As an employee herself, Zoe wondered how the rest of the staff viewed her inclusion in the party. But then, her position was hardly the same, was it? She was treated by all as one of the family.

David sat up front with Alexis when they left, leaving the three women to occupy the rear seats. Zoe was grateful to have Sofia between her and Christa, although she knew that sooner or later she would be faced with an inquisition as to the exact nature of her relationship with Alexis. The woman was neither blind nor stupid; she knew there was something going on.

Not that Zoe had any intention of telling her anything. With another two days, or even more, of uncertainty to get through, Christa's sentiments were the least of her worries.

CHAPTER SEVEN

THE roads were busy despite the lighter holiday traffic, and it was almost half-past nine before they finally reached the port.

At a hundred and thirty feet, the *Hestia* was among the larger of the private yachts, and of a classic design that incorporated superb, deeply varnished teak and polished brass along with its traditional scrubbed decks. Captain Dimitris Dragoumis welcomed them aboard. He was in his late forties, and treated Alexis with the deference due to the owner without relinquishing any of his own air of command. Zoe liked him on sight.

Below, the yacht was equipped with all the modern comforts one could desire. Her cabin had a double bed, flanked by built-in cupboards and drawer units, with a small but beautifully appointed bathroom en suite. In any other circumstances, she would have considered herself blessed by the gods themselves to be here at all. This was living with a capital L!

Sofia was right next door in a cabin much the same.

'I love being on board the *Hestia* too,' she agreed when Zoe expressed her appreciation. 'She was completely refitted six years ago when Alexis first acquired her. He's considered buying a more modern yacht from time to time, but he always decides against it in the end. I hope he keeps the *Hestia* until she falls to pieces!'

'Which won't be for a long time yet, I imagine,' Zoe responded. 'She's so beautifully maintained.'

'Captain Dimitris makes sure of that. He loves the *Hestia* as if she were his own. She'll be out to charter for the whole of June and July as usual.'

To help defray running expenses, Zoe imagined. Considering the size of the crew alone, they must run to a small fortune. Another world indeed!

The main deck held a roomy and comfortably furnished saloon, with a dining saloon opening off it, the two of which could be combined, via sliding doors, to form one huge entertaining space. Glass doors gave access to the open aft deck set out with padded loungers and chairs, and containing a small round swimming-pool that could be covered in the evenings to allow dancing if required.

Curtained window ports in the superstructure, jutting forward of and below the bridge, outlined the owner's stateroom, with Alexis presumably in residence at the moment. Zoe resisted the impulse to glance in as Sofia led the way round to the starboard side, where they mounted a short gangway leading to yet another sundeck aft of the bridge housing.

The young and exceptionally handsome crew member, plumping up cushions in the lounging area, offered a cheerful greeting, totally uninhibited by Sofia's status as sister of the owner. It was, Zoe understood him to say, going to be an exceptionally good voyage. From the sparkle in his eyes as he looked the two of them over she concluded that Sofia's and her presence alone would make it so for him. She was unsurprised to learn that his name was Adonis.

'He's new this year,' said Sofia after he had departed with reluctance to fulfil other duties. She was sparkling herself. 'I'm so happy to be here—especially with you, Zoe. You cannot imagine how much!'

'Having your brother and sister together for two or three weeks must be nice too,' replied Zoe lightly. 'I'm looking forward to meeting your other relatives on Santorini. Are they on your mother's or your father's side of the family?'

'Father's. Grandfather came to Athens many years ago. He was quite poor to begin with, I think, but he had a good head for business. One which both Father and Alexis inherited. The brother left on Santorini was content to stay there. His two sons—my father's cousins—still live on the island with their families.'

'And you've kept in touch all these years?'

'Yes, although Alexis was the one to renew close ties again. They are very different from our relatives here in Athens.'

They would have to be, Zoe reflected, to be worth the trouble being taken to see them.

The two couples who were to make up the party arrived together around eleven. They were around Alexis's own age group, and of a disposition that soon did away with any fears Zoe had entertained of being made to feel out of things.

She had suspected that Orestes Antoniou might have been invited along too, although his name hadn't been mentioned. It was possible, she supposed, that she had been reading the whole thing wrong from the start. That Alexis hadn't seen fit to repudiate the suggestion, if so, meant only that he considered it none of her business anyway.

They sailed at noon, heading for the island of Sifnos, where they would make their first call, before threading their way down to Santorini on the extreme edge of the group. Standing at the port rail, Zoe watched the coastline slip by, disconcerted to be joined there by David Townsend.

'Ever done any of the islands before?' he asked casually.

'Only Hydra and Poros,' she admitted. 'And hardly in the same style. Have you?'

He shook his head. 'This is my first time aboard the *Hestia* too. I wouldn't be here now if Christa hadn't brought pressure to bear.' His smile robbed the words of any hidden gibe. 'It's the first real holiday I've taken in two years, so I suppose she had a point.'

'What do you do?' asked Zoe.

'I'm in banking,' he said. 'The commercial variety.'

'Chairman?' she hazarded, and he laughed.

'Not quite. The present incumbent looks set until retirement, which won't be for another five years. I might run then, if I get the backing.' He gave her a sideways glance. 'I shouldn't have thought playing nursemaid to Sofia stretched *your* capabilities very far.'

She stiffened a fraction. 'I'm not a nursemaid.'

'Companion, then. It amounts to the same thing. Not that you're not doing a good job. I can see a big difference in my sister-in-law since the last time I was over. She used to be so reserved.' The smile came again. 'If Christa had been the same, we'd probably never have got together.'

'She must have been very much in love with you,' Zoe murmured softly, 'to leave her family and country the way she did.'

'No more than I with her. We were given no choice. Her father refused even to meet me. She came to me in the end with only the clothes she was wearing at the time because he was going to send her to stay with his uncle on Santorini until she came to her senses. That was the last she ever saw of him—and of her mother too, of course. You knew she died when Sofia was born?'

'Yes.' Zoe was silent for a moment, visualising the younger Christa, prepared to sacrifice everything for love of a man, and wondering if she could have done the same in the Greek woman's circumstances. 'It must have been a happy day for her when Alexis put the whole thing aside.'

'It was. He's quite a guy, as the Yanks would say.' The pause held a certain deliberation. 'There's something going on between you two, isn't there?'

Zoe felt her stomach muscles form themselves into a tight knot. She could tell David to mind his own business, but that would be tantamount to admitting the truth in what he was saying. She forced herself to stay calm and collected, at least on the surface.

'I think you might be reading a lot into a little. Alexis tends to act as if I, as well as Sofia, am his responsibility, but he has no other interest in me.'

David gave her a steady appraisal that took in the cloud of bright hair and widely spaced green eyes. 'He's interested, all right. He was like a cat on hot bricks when you got lost on Saturday night. I can understand his feeling that way. You're a very attractive young woman. I'd just hate to see you get hurt, that's all.'

'Why?' she asked on a harder note. 'You don't even know me.' She swung her head to look back at him, casting discretion aside in sudden surging resentment. 'Your wife put you up to this, didn't she? Well, you can tell her that if anything was going on between her brother and me it would be our affair and no one else's!'

She left him standing there, already regretting the outburst as she made her way forward. The sight of Alexis himself descending the gangway from the bridge brought her up short in consternation at the thought that he might have overheard, but if he had he gave no sign.

'I was coming to look for you,' he said.

'It's too soon,' she claimed fiercely. 'I already told you that! Just leave me alone, will you?'

His jaw clenched. 'I've no intention of doing that. And don't even consider attempting to lie to me, should you not receive the proof you need, because I'll know!'

Conscious of the man still standing at the rail some short distance away, Zoe took a hold on herself. 'The thought hadn't crossed my mind,' she said on a more restrained note. That was a lie in itself, but she felt no guilt. The very idea of discussing her bodily functions this way was anathema to her. 'I'm going below,' she added. 'I'd like to be on my own for a while, if that isn't asking too much.'

'As you wish.' Alexis stood aside to allow her passage, his eyes revealing the anger still seething within him. 'We should reach Sifnos by early evening, so there'll be time to go ashore. Wear something suitable in which to clamber in and out of the boat that will take us to land.'

Zoe made her escape almost before he had finished speaking. The way she felt at the moment, going ashore held little appeal. Telephoning home yesterday, she had found it difficult to filter the concern from her voice. Her mother had been moved at one point to ask if there was anything wrong. She'd denied it, of course, but had gained the impression that she was only half believed.

Both her parents would be terribly hurt if she did turn out to be pregnant, she thought miserably. Neither of them were what you might call modern thinkers when it came to such matters—any more, it appeared, than was Alexis himself.

She and Sofia spent the afternoon sunbathing on the upper deck, leaving the others to their own devices. From the hum of conversation filtering up from the aft deck, it seemed that most of them were congregated there. Sofia must feel at times that she was destined to spend her life with people older than herself, Zoe reflected.

'Do you ever think about marriage, Sofia?' she asked casually.

'Of course,' came the ready reply. 'All girls think about marriage. I want no less than four children!'

Zoe shut off that train of thought before it could get going. 'And for a husband?'

'Orestes Antoniou would be Alexis's choice of a suitable husband for me.'

'Not your own?'

There was a brief pause before the answer. 'He is *very* suitable.'

'But you don't love him?'

'I'm not sure,' said Sofia consideringly, 'that love is of such great importance. Not when compared with other matters. There are many who would consider themselves well blessed to have Orestes Antoniou wish to marry them.'

'Don't do it,' Zoe begged. 'He's not worthy of you. You're only just eighteen. You've all the time in the world!'

'Not if I want to have my children before I become too old to enjoy them—or even to be with them. My mother was old when she had me, and see what happened to her.'

'She could only have been in her late thirties,' Zoe protested. 'That isn't old. Complications can arise at any age.'

'But there is far less chance of it at nineteen or twenty.' Sofia sounded unusually dogged. 'And who else should I marry? So far as I'm aware, Alexis has received no other approach.'

'That isn't to say there won't be others.' Zoe was sitting up with her hands clasped about her bent knees. 'Even if you think love isn't essential, you surely have to at least *like* the man? You didn't give me the impression you liked Orestes all that much the day he called on you.'

This time the pause was lengthier, culminating in a sigh. 'No, I don't. He thinks far too much of himself.' She gave a sudden giggle. 'He and Leda would make a fine pair!'

She was still a child in many ways, thought Zoe fondly. Only a child could turn so quickly from despondency to mirth. If she had managed to talk her out of accepting a future in which Orestes Antoniou figured, that was all to the good. As to the latter observation, Leda Kazantzi was the last person Zoe herself wanted to think about at present.

Set on a mountainous inlet, with twin chapels crowning its flanking summits, the little port of Kamares was still enjoying the relative peace and quiet of a season only just getting under way. Come July and August, when the inter-island ferries were running to full capacity, the tamarisk-shaded bars and restaurants strung along the waterside would be chock-a-block, the harbour itself awash with craft of all shapes and sizes, but for now, Zoe thought, it couldn't be more pleasant.

They had taken a couple of tables at a taverna situated where the harbour gave way to beach. She could see the lights of the *Hestia*, lying at anchor about a quarter of a mile out. The decision to eat dinner ashore had been Alexis's. They wouldn't be sailing again until morning.

The two Greek couples had enough English to enable conversation to be carried on primarily in that language. Zoe felt uncomfortable that her presence made the concession necessary, but her Greek was still too sparse for any but the most simple phrases to be understood. She had deliberately chosen a seat that enabled her to avoid catching Alexis's eye at any point. It was difficult enough acting the part of the carefree holiday-maker without any added strain.

Seated directly opposite, Christa was oddly quiet and introspective. Zoe couldn't be sure whether David had passed on the message she had sent or not. Whichever, he didn't seem to bear her any ill-will for the rebuff. If anything, he seemed to set himself out to be friendly.

The food was excellent, the wine plentiful. Stuffed to the gills with succulent red mullet and feta cheese salad, washed down with several glasses of the fine Côtes de Melithon that had been produced in triumph by the proprietor on Alexis's request, Zoe managed to cast her problems aside for the evening and join in the general spirit of *bonhomie*.

The entertainment began quite spontaneously with one of the locals plucking a *bouzouki* while another sang one of the hauntingly melancholy themes known as *rebetika*. It was all about a lost son, as far as Zoe could translate, and brought her close to tears. She was becoming a real weepy, she thought wryly, glad when the song ended.

The taverna was full to overflowing by now, the various parties merging as extra chairs and tables were procured. More musicians arrived to add to the general atmosphere of joyful abandon. Following some inner compulsion, one of the men got to his feet and performed a solo dance, lost in a world of his own as he moved with eyes riveted to the floor and arms outstretched. No one applauded when he finished, nor did he seem to expect it, returning to his seat to join in conversation as if there had been no interruption.

She loved the Greeks *en masse*, thought Zoe mistily. They had such a zest for life, such a total lack of self-consciousness. Moved by the same inner spirit, Alexis himself was more Greek tonight than she had ever known him, his face animated as he talked, laughter unrestrained. She loved him so much, it hurt to even think about it.

It was the early hours of the morning before they returned to the yacht. She would pay for the amount of wine she had drunk, Zoe knew, but at present she felt as if she were floating on air.

Lying in a bed that rocked gently backwards and forwards to the movement of the water was a pleasant sensation. She drifted off into a fantasy in which Alexis was declaring that he loved her and couldn't live without her; that he wanted her more than any other woman in the world!

As on that other occasion, the realisation that the arms about her were real, that the lips claiming hers were no figment of a dream made no difference to her responses. She kissed him back hungrily, feverishly, everything else blanked out but for this overpowering need to be with him, a part of him. His hands were so wonderfully sure, inducing a quivering expectancy. She was on fire with love for him, with desire for him.

The opening of the cabin door went unnoted by them both. It took Sofia's voice to drag them up from the depths.

'I thought I heard you call out,' she said. 'Are you——?' The words died in her throat as she took in the fact that there was more than one person in the bed. There was enough light from the uncovered port to reveal the identity of that other occupant too. His name came from her lips in stunned disbelief. 'Alexis!'

She had backed out and shut the door again before either of them could react. Shocked into total and sickening sobriety, Zoe lay for a brief frozen moment before making a violent move to push Alexis away.

'I must go after her,' she gasped wildly. 'I must explain!'

'Explain what?' he asked on a low, rough note. 'She isn't a child. She knows what she saw. It isn't the way I would have wanted her to learn about us, but the damage is done.'

'It wouldn't have been if you'd left me alone the way I asked you to!' she accused with a vehemence that owed much to her own guilty conscience. 'You just can't take no for an answer, can you?'

'You weren't telling me no a few moments ago,' came the harsh rejoinder. 'Apportioning blame isn't going to help matters.' He rose abruptly from the bed to move across to the port, blocking out the moonlight as he stood gazing out.

He was wearing one of the white towelling bathrobes provided in his and her sizes in every cabin. The bareness of his legs below suggested that that was *all* he was wearing. Zoe felt her throat tauten painfully.

'Does Sifnos have an airport?' she asked in desperation, and he turned to look back at her.

'Why?'

'I can't face Sofia again after this. It would be best all round if I just disappeared!'

His mouth twisted. 'Leaving me to face her alone?' He gave her no time to reply. 'Even if air transport were available, you wouldn't be taking it. In the morning we announce our forthcoming marriage. It won't remove the blemish, but it will mitigate it.'

Zoe sat bolt upright. 'You can't do that!'

It was impossible from this distance and in so little light to read the expression in his eyes—or even to know if there was one. 'You'll have the opportunity to deny it if you wish. For now, I think it best that I leave you.'

She could find neither will nor words to keep him there. With the door closed in his wake, she collapsed slowly back into the pillows, feeling caught between the devil and the deep blue sea. That had been no idle declaration; Sofia's respect had to be regained, no matter at what cost. To repudiate the announcement in front of her would be the most difficult thing Zoe had ever done, but do it, she must—for all their sakes.

Sleep came eventually through sheer exhaustion. She awoke at eight, heavy-eyed and with a banging headache.

They were under way, she realised, feeling the throbbing of the engines.

Memory returned with dispiriting clarity. She had to force herself to get up. The discovery that pregnancy was definitely out brought mixed emotions: on the one hand was relief, on the other despondency, and she wasn't at all sure which was the greater. Not that it made a great deal of difference anyway if Alexis kept his word.

Aspirin went some way towards reducing the headache, but did nothing at all for her emotional state. She found the rest of the party out on the after-deck, drinking coffee, when she finally nerved herself to go up. Alexis was talking with David, and didn't immediately notice her arrival, while Sofia studiously avoided meeting her eyes.

Noting it, Christa gave Zoe a sharply questioning glance, which the latter fended as best as she was able. She refused coffee, and concentrated instead on the sea-scape astern.

Sifnos was a low-lying blob on the horizon, soon to be lost from view entirely. Later they would pass between Sikinos and Folegandros to land at Santorini mid-afternoon. They were to stay there two days before heading south again for Crete. Where they were to go after that, she didn't yet know. The itinerary was flexible. Sofia had mentioned Rhodes at one point.

She could see Alexis out of the corner of her eye. He had finished his conversation with David, and was sitting in quiet contemplation of his coffee-cup. It was possible, she supposed, that he had changed his mind about the whole affair. Where Alexis was concerned, anything was possible.

She went first hot and then cold when he looked up and in her direction. Even from this angle, the decisiveness in his expression was not to be mistaken. Then he was getting to his feet, and coming across to draw her to hers, eyes issuing a warning as he bent his head to kiss her lightly on the lips before turning her to face the startled assembly with a proprietorial arm about her shoulders.

He made the announcement in Greek, but Zoe had no difficulty at all in understanding the words herself. She had done him the honour, he said, of consenting to become his wife. Just that, nothing more.

Standing there at his side, watching the varied reactions, she felt oddly detached from it all. From initial shock and confusion, Sofia's expression began to register a cautious relief as she gazed at the two of them—a sentiment scarcely echoed by her sister, who simply looked stunned. Of the rest, only David managed to gather himself for an immediate response, his voice over-hearty as he offered congratulations.

'You certainly didn't waste any time making up your minds,' he added with jocularity. 'Love at first sight, was it?'

'If not quite the first, certainly the second,' Alexis conceded. He sounded, Zoe thought, amazingly light-hearted about it. His glance moved to his elder sister. 'We have you to thank for bringing us together, Christa. If you hadn't seen fit to take a hand in Sofia's welfare we'd never have met. Isn't that so, *agapi mou*?' The last with a squeeze of the arm holding Zoe close by his side.

Agapi mou meant darling, that part of her brain still functioning properly supplied. Or, more precisely, *my* darling. Only he didn't mean it. He didn't mean any of it. The whole thing had been forced on him. The fact that it was by circumstances of his own making was neither here nor there.

Christa made a startlingly speedy recovery. 'I'll have to change my name to Eros,' she said. 'Congratulations, both of you.'

Sofia came over and kissed Zoe on the cheek. 'I'm so glad!' she murmured. The embrace she offered her brother was equally restrained—more, Zoe felt, from embarrassment than reproof. 'I hope you will be very happy.'

If she had ever really intended renouncing the idea, the time was past and gone, acknowledged Zoe fatalistically. For now, at any rate. Much as she thought of Sofia, she couldn't go through with this marriage for her sake alone. Once this cruise was over the whole matter would have to be straightened out.

'Is the wedding to be in Athens or England?' asked one of the other women.

'A matter still to be decided,' Alexis answered without turning a hair. 'I've yet to meet Zoe's family.'

Christa was looking at Zoe with a faintly puzzled expression. 'You're very quiet,' she commented.

'It's all happened so quickly,' returned Zoe with truth. 'I'm still having trouble believing it.'

'I'm no figment of imagination,' claimed Alexis on a note of amusement. 'And it happened no more quickly than for Christa and David.'

'That's true.' His sister's tone had softened reminiscently, her eyes briefly seeking those of her husband. 'We both of us knew the moment we met.' She stood up and came over to embrace first Zoe and then her brother with what appeared to be genuine approval. 'I'm happy for you!'

I'm being drawn ever deeper, thought Zoe helplessly. Christa's blessing was the least expected. Between her and Sofia—to say nothing of Alexis himself—she felt trapped.

CHAPTER EIGHT

THE morning was gone before Zoe managed to secure a few private minutes with Alexis. She did it by following him to his cabin when the whole group adjourned to refresh themselves before lunch, nerving herself against the urge to leave it all for another time as she tapped lightly on the bulkhead door.

He looked surprised to see her standing there, and indicated that she should come in, closing the door again to regard her steadily.

'If you came to tell me you don't wish to marry me, you're too late,' he declared. 'The time to voice any objection was at the moment of announcement.'

'You made that impossible,' she said. She paused, searching for the right words, finding none but the bare statement of fact. 'I'm not pregnant.'

There was a flash of some emotion too swiftly come and gone in the dark eyes to be defined. 'So?'

Zoe was nonplussed by the calm acceptance. She said slowly, 'You have to feel some relief.'

There was a hint of irony in his faint smile. 'To learn that I'm not quite as virile as I might have believed?'

'Only a man,' she flashed, 'would look at it that way!'

'And I,' he agreed, 'am a man. No matter. There'll be time enough.'

'But there's no longer any need to go through with it,' she said. 'We're stuck with the situation for the moment, admittedly, but later we can announce that we rushed into the whole thing too fast, and call it off.'

Alexis continued to regard her with the same unreadable expression. 'I've no intention of calling it off, as you so eloquently put it. As the first man to know you, I have the honour of the Theodorou name to uphold.'

'That's ridiculous!' The protest was impassioned. 'I can't be the first virgin you ever made love to!'

'Yes, you are.' It was said quietly but with no less positivity. 'And I cannot and will not allow that any other man should follow me.'

Possessiveness, she reminded herself, not love. All the same, it meant something. The temptation to give in and go with the flow was strong. If family honour really meant so much to him...

As if recognising the indecision, he moved forward to take her in his arms and find her mouth with his in a kiss that reached deep into her heart. He could be so gentle when he wanted to be—so infinitely sensitive.

He held her face between his palms while he pressed feather-light kisses on her eyes and then to the fluttering pulse at each temple. His lips were delicate in their slow passage down her cheek and along the line of her jaw to seek her mouth again. Zoe could feel herself trembling deep down inside—feel the emotion flooding every part of her. Whether he loved her or not, she loved him. More than she had thought it possible to love any man. How could she possibly turn her back on it all?

'You belong to me,' he said very softly when he finally desisted. 'It may not be quite so imperative any longer that we marry in haste, but marry we must. As soon as we return to Athens we'll both of us go and tell your parents. Is that agreed?'

Zoe was beyond further denial. 'It's agreed.'

'Then we understand each other at last.' There was a certain wryness about the line of his mouth as he released her. 'Passion must be contained for the present.'

No more than three or four days, if she ran true to form, she wanted to tell him, but that kind of intimacy was outside her limits as yet.

Up until this moment, she hadn't taken any real note of her surroundings. The state-room was lined throughout in teak and maple panelling, with furnishings in the same wood. A king-size bed, set within an alcove created by built-in wardrobes, had covers in cream slub silk to match the port curtains, while the carpet underfoot was a deeper cream wool that felt inches thick.

'The glass is one-way,' advised Alexis, seeing her expression undergo an abrupt alteration as she glanced once more at the large square ports. 'No one can see in. The other state-room is equal in size, if you'd prefer to be below decks when we next sail together.'

He meant as man and wife, Zoe assumed. Perhaps even a honeymoon trip? The thought alone increased her pulse-rate.

She said reluctantly, 'I'd better go and get ready for lunch. We'll need to have finished eating before we reach Santorini.'

'We can always stand off until we're ready to go ashore,' came the dry reply. 'Dimitris follows my time-table, not his own.'

Zoe could well imagine. Dimitris Dragoumis might be captain of the *Hestia*, but Alexis was master. He would expect to be hers too when they were married, which was something else to raise doubts as to the probability of it ever working out. Love him as she did, there was no way she could accept the role of subservient.

Showered and dressed again in white cotton trousers and sleeveless top, she hesitated for a moment outside Sofia's cabin door before deciding to get it over with. The invitation to enter came in Greek.

There was little welcome in the younger girl's expression when she saw who her visitor was. Zoe had the feeling that she had been expecting her sister.

'I need to talk with you,' she said. 'You must have a very low opinion of me after last night.'

The smooth olive skin took on sudden heat. 'It was very…embarrassing. I know, of course, that such things happen between men and women——' She broke off, eyes searching Zoe's with intensity. 'Do you and Alexis *have* to marry?'

Zoe was grateful that she could at least set her mind at rest on that score. 'I'm not pregnant, if that's what you mean.'

The relief was obvious. 'Then it can only be for love! Even so, Alexis should have been prepared to wait until you were his wife before giving way to his urges.'

'It takes two,' Zoe responded gently, allowing the misapprehension to pass. 'He used no force.'

'But he is a man, and men are skilled in the art of seduction.'

The parrot-fashion pronouncement drew a faint smile to Zoe's lips. 'Who taught you that one?'

'It is,' came the serious reply, 'a fact of life against which all of our sex have need to guard.' She gave vent to a small sigh. 'I feel so much happier now I know that you and Alexis really love each other. I could ask for no one I'd rather have for a sister-in-law!'

'Not even Leda Kazantzi?' asked Zoe, striving for a light note.

Sofia laughed. 'I'd love to see her face when she hears the news! She'll have to find someone else to marry her.'

Which shouldn't be difficult, Zoe reflected, with her looks. She must have dozens of admirers to choose from. None, perhaps, filling the bill quite as well as Alexis had, but that she would simply have to accept.

Alexis looked pleased to see her and Sofia on apparently easy terms with each other again over lunch. It left only Christa to be faced now, although the other showed no sign of ill-will. No further mention was made of the forthcoming wedding, for which Zoe was grateful. She had enough on her plate, thinking about what she was going to tell her parents.

A letter would be better than a phone call, she decided. If she posted it from, say, Crete, they would have had time to get over the initial shock before she got back to Athens. Her mother hadn't even liked her coming here for a year. How she was going to feel about a permanent residency wasn't difficult to guess. Zoe didn't find it easy to think in those terms either. Much as she enjoyed this country and its people, it wasn't home.

Seen from a distance, the two brilliant white villages topping the crescent-shaped island looked like icing on a giant chocolate cake. The thousand-foot cliffs became streaked with reds and browns and the white of pumice stone as they drew nearer, the 'icing' resolving itself into church domes and cubist houses, crowding the rim of what had once been part of the volcanic crater before the massive eruption thousands of years ago had split the island apart.

Studying the scene, Zoe wondered if she really was looking at what remained of the lost Atlantis. Whether or not, there was a forbidding air about the towering, barren cliffs.

'The islets there still have active craters,' advised Alexis, standing by her at the rail. 'They're called *Kamenae*, which means burned ones.'

'There was a big earthquake here in the fifties, wasn't there?' she asked. 'How did your relatives fare?'

'They survived.'

'But it could happen again?'

Broad shoulders lifted in an expressive shrug. 'Possibly. Unlikely, though, that it should do so during the next two days.'

The thought had crossed her mind, Zoe had to admit. Perched the way it was up there, Phira was hardly what one might call a secure location.

'I couldn't live with a threat like that hanging over me,' she declared with a shiver. 'I think your cousins are very brave to stay.'

'They're involved in the tourist industry,' he said, as if that explained everything. 'A hotel and restaurant. We'll be staying there ourselves for two nights.' He straightened as the anchor went down with a rattle. 'We'd normally have disembarked at Athinios and driven up to Phira the back way, but I thought you might like to take the telecabin up from the old port.'

'I'd rather go by mule,' claimed Zoe, following the zig-zag line of the roadway snaking up the cliff-side. 'I've always wanted to do that. I could meet you at the top.'

'I'll come with you,' offered Sofia. 'I find it fun too.'

Alexis's smile was indulgent. 'Not the way I would describe it myself, but an experience, yes. The boat is here to take us ashore.'

Stepping into the small rocking craft from the gangway platform was no simple task. Zoe was glad of Alexis's supporting arm. He sat alongside her during the crossing to the narrow stone quayside, which crouched along the base of the cliffs, one arm draped along the gunwale at her back.

The vivid blue of the sky, the sombre, yet ever-changing colours of the bare rock, the glowing warmth of the sun were all part and parcel of the sudden bubbling happiness she felt. Home was where the heart was, and hers was right here with Alexis.

Passengers had already been ferried ashore from the cruise liner that had dropped anchor just before them.

The last of those who had chosen to make the upward journey on mule or donkey-back in preference to the modern cable-car was just leaving the mounting-block. Donkey-drivers surrounded the new party, hustling for business in much the same way as the quayside traders and room touts on other islands.

Alexis settled a price with the minimum of fuss, and saw the two of them mounted on a pair of sad-looking donkeys, which, he declared firmly, were likely to be a steadier ride than the mules.

Steady was the word, Zoe conceded, as her own mount began to plod an uncomplaining passage up the wide stairs that formed the roadway. Some of the people just up ahead looked far too big and heavy for the mounts they had been allocated, although the animals themselves seemed to be managing all right.

The driver coming up behind used a switch to urge her donkey into faster movement. He looked surprised when she asked him to stop, but did so anyway, shrugging his shoulders in tolerant recognition of her misplaced sympathies. If anyone deserved commiseration, she could imagine him thinking, it was surely the man himself, forced to walk this long and weary road in the heat of the afternoon instead of whiling away the siesta hours in time-honoured fashion.

The view, as they rose, grew ever more tremendous. With two smaller, though no less precipitous islands forming an opposing wall to the west, it was possible to visualise the extent of the original crater. From here the sea looked peacock-blue, stretching as far as the eye could reach.

A sudden clatter of hoofs and shouts from up ahead signalled a descending group. They were coming fast, Zoe saw in alarm as the leading animals rounded the switchback bend. Her own mount moved over automatically to make room, and she found herself looking straight down a five-hundred-foot drop into the sea. Clutching frantically at the pommel, she squeezed her eyes shut until the down-coming file had passed and there was room once again to swing clear of the edge. She could only hope and pray that they wouldn't be meeting any more like that.

Her knees felt more than a little wobbly when they finally alighted at around the five-hundredth stair. There were more stairs to climb into the town itself, but she was glad to do them on foot in order to regain her sense of balance. Sofia reacted with sympathy when she admitted how petrified she had been for those few moments. Accidents, the Greek girl said, were extremely rare.

Tourist shops selling all manner of goods flanked the upper reaches of the staircase. Alexis was waiting for them at the top. The others, he said, had gone straight to the hotel.

'I think it might be a good idea if we sat for a while over a drink before we join them,' he observed when Sofia told him of Zoe's scare. 'Had I known you suffered from vertigo, I'd never have allowed you to make the journey!'

'I don't,' Zoe denied. 'Not normally. I think it was being on the donkey that did it. Its hoofs were right on the edge!'

'They're very sure footed animals,' he said. 'Whatever the cause, we take no more such risks.'

What was with this 'we' business? she thought in a sudden flash of resentment. She was capable of deciding for herself!

The pique was renewed when they took a table on the open terrace of a taverna overlooking the magnificent view, and Alexis insisted that she sit on the side furthest away from the balustrade.

'I'm quite recovered,' she said, attempting to treat the matter lightly. 'It's blondes who are supposed to be dizzy, not redheads!'

'It would have been no joking matter had you fallen from the saddle back there,' he returned unsmilingly. 'I would never have forgiven myself.'

Looking at him, Zoe felt rancour give way to the softer, deeper emotion. She was being petty, and for what? All he was doing was showing that he cared what happened to her. She should be thankful for it, not resentful.

He ordered coffee for them all, adding something to the waiter that Zoe didn't catch. The cup of French-style filter coffee placed before her several minutes later was a delightful surprise. It was available for the tourists, Alexis said dismissively when she thanked him for the thought, making her feel like one herself. He hadn't meant it that way, she was sure, but it still rankled. Would there ever come a time, she wondered bleakly, when she would truly belong in this world of his?

The *Hestia* was no longer at anchor in the bay. She had sailed for Athinios, a few miles south, from where their luggage would be brought by car up the back route that Alexis had spoken of earlier. The cliffs just here were not as sheer, allowing the town to spill over in a multitude of different levels reached by threaded staircases. Geraniums graced almost every window-ledge in splashes of brilliant red against sun-kissed white.

'I love it here!' declared Sofia contentedly, drawing her brother's speculative glance.

'You'd like to stay on?'

She laughed. 'I love it to visit, not to live.' Her expression underwent a sudden alteration. 'Unless you would prefer to have Mimosa to yourselves when you are married?'

'Apart from the staff, you mean?' asked Zoe smilingly when Alexis made no immediate reply. 'It wouldn't be the same without you.'

The younger girl relaxed again. 'Nor for me without you now. It will be good to have a sister close to me. I see so little of Christa.'

'Perhaps,' Zoe suggested purposefully, 'we'll be able to visit her in England.' She cast a glance at Alexis, more than half expecting to see dissension in the dark eyes. 'Yes?'

There was a hint of mockery in the inclination of his head. 'It could well be.'

Sofia's face was lit from within. 'That will be wonderful!'

Asking, Zoe acknowledged, was going to get her a lot further than demanding, although it still rankled a little to play up to the male ego that way. The best way of handling it was to make a game of it, she supposed—until it came to something really important. She could hardly spend her life arguing minor issues just for the sake of it.

The Hotel Apollon was situated up towards the imposing cathedral, and overlooked the same fantastic view. With twenty rooms and a roof-top restaurant, it commanded a 'C' class rating, which Zoe knew from past experience usually signified a more than satisfactory standard of comfort.

Alexis was greeted with typical Greek enthusiasm by his cousin Stavros and his wife Chariklia, who had already dispatched the rest of the party to their respective rooms. Sofia was embraced like a long-lost daughter of the house. Drawn forward by Alexis, Zoe prepared herself for the inevitable reaction when he introduced her as his future wife, but the surprise was short-lived, the delight obviously genuine. Whatever Alexis chose to do, she gathered, was fine with them.

The whole family, including the other cousin, Costas, appeared to be involved in the business. Zoe became confused as to whose was which in the various sons and daughters called forth from their duties for inspection. Costas's wife was named Merope, and she apparently did all the cooking. She had planned a special menu for them tonight, she declared. All of them could speak English to some degree, but they expressed the usual pleasure at Zoe's efforts to use their own language.

The room to which she was eventually shown was basic by British standards, but sparkling clean and neat. A bed with hand-crocheted cover stood opposite the glass window-door, which gave on to a tiny balcony. A dressing-chest and wardrobe completed the main furnishings. Off to the side, a further door led through to a minute shower-room and toilet.

'It's lovely,' she assured the anxiously hovering Chariklia. '*Oreo*!'

The other beamed at the compliment, assured Zoe in English that their home was her home while ever she was here, and returned to her duties, whatever they were, downstairs.

Pushing open the glass door, Zoe stepped out on to the balcony to drink in the stunning scenery once more. The sun was lowering towards the two islands on the other side of the *caldera*, a great golden orb soon to be extinguished in the sea. There was a smell of sulphur in the air, though hardly strong enough to be unpleasant. The sound of music filtered up from somewhere among the tumbled terraces below.

Alexis appeared in the doorway behind her. 'I knocked,' he said, 'but there was no answer. Is everything to your satisfaction?'

'You sound like a hotel proprietor yourself,' she teased, turning to smile at him. 'Everything is wonderful!'

'*Everything*?' he repeated softly.

She had a sense of burning all her boats behind her as she answered equally softly, 'Yes.'

He took her by the hand and drew her back into the room, held her close for a long, heart-warming moment before kissing her. There was no doubting his physical desire for her, Zoe thought tremulously as his lips moved on down the length of her throat to find the pulse throbbing at its base. He made no secret of it. She caught at his hands as he began unfastening the buttons of her cotton shirt.

'Alexis . . .'

'I hadn't forgotten,' he said. 'I want to hold you in my arms, nothing more.'

Not *just* sex, then, came the comforting thought. Few men, from what she had heard and read, understood a woman's need of tender succour at such times as this. She hadn't been fully appreciative of it herself until this moment.

She made no further attempt to stop him from taking off the shirt and the lacy bra beneath. Her whole body tremored as he cupped one achingly full breast in his palm and bent to press his lips to it. She tangled her fingers in the black pelt of his hair, loving the springy feel of it—so vital with life, like the man himself.

'The door,' she murmured huskily when he lifted his head. 'Sofia might——'

'Sofia is downstairs with our cousins,' he said. 'And the door is locked.' He held her a little away from him, eyes black as night as he studied the firm, tautly peaked curves. 'So very lovely, *agapi mou.*'

The same endearment he had used before, yet so much more meaningful here and now. Instinct moved her to unbutton his own shirt and slide it back over the broad shoulders, to bury her lips in the tight swirls of hair covering his chest, to fill her nostrils with the erotic male scent of him and taste the faint saltiness of his skin.

Alexis lifted her and laid her on the bed, then came down alongside her to kiss her with all the tender passion she craved. His lips were a source of endless pleasure, carrying her to a peak of fulfilment that inspired a need to do the same for him. He lay there watching her through hooded lids while she removed the rest of his clothing, his body totally still as she began the tentative exploration.

His skin was smooth and firm, the muscle dormant. Zoe lost herself in the sheer feel of him, sliding her hand over one powerful shoulder and along the length of his arm, then back again to follow the line of his chest down to the hard-ridged stomach and taut waist. Flat and hard, the male hip was so different from a woman's, the thighs so much stronger and solid.

He was already fully and vibrantly aroused. She felt the shudder run through him at her touch, heard the harshly indrawn breath and knew a sudden heady sense of her own power. Proud, arrogant, forceful though he might be, at this moment he was all hers.

The setting sun was casting a deep orange glow into the room when he finally left her. By the time Zoe had showered and dressed, it was dark.

The single overhead bulb left much of the room in shadow. She had to turn the small mirror standing on the chest of drawers sideways in order to see her reflection clearly enough to apply lipstick and just a touch of mascara. Her face looked no different, apart, perhaps, from a certain added glow in her eyes; it was only inside that any real transfiguration had taken place. If she couldn't make Alexis love her in quite the same way that she loved him, she could settle for what they had. It was more than many would ever know.

That evening was one of the best she had ever spent. True to her word, Merope had produced a feast fit for a king. They began with the *yaprak dolmathes*, consisting of vine leaves wrapped around a stuffing of savoury mince and rice, followed by *giuvetsi*, which turned out to be roast spring lamb and pasta cooked and served in individual earthenware dishes. The wine was local and powerful. Zoe confined herself to the one glass, plumping for the Greek yoghurt made from sheep's milk to finish the meal; laced with honey, it was absolutely delicious.

'I think,' she said lightly to Christa, who was seated next to her, 'that I could all too easily get fat, eating like this all the time!'

'I doubt it,' came the dry return. 'You aren't the type to allow yourself to become indifferent to the way you look.'

The others were all involved in conversations of their own. Zoe took advantage of the moment to make an approach to the woman who was to become her sister-in-law. 'I really didn't *plan* for this to happen, you know.'

The smile was unexpected. 'I believe you. Alexis would never have allowed himself to be drawn into a liaison against his will. What I said to you that first evening was meant only to save you from hurt. I failed to recognise the depth of Alexis's feelings for you.'

Hardly surprising, Zoe thought. Aloud, she said, 'I'm sorry about Leda Kazantzi.'

Christa gave a brief shrug. 'Where there are winners, there also have to be losers. Leda is resilient. She'll get over Alexis.'

'She really loves him?'

'Why should you doubt it? *You* love him.' The older woman gave her a sharp glance. 'At least, I take it you do?'

Seated at the far end of the long table, and deep in discussion with the other men, Alexis was unlikely to overhear anything said at this end, Zoe calculated.

Hardly important anyway. He had to know by now how she felt about him.

'Of course,' she confirmed. 'I wouldn't be marrying him otherwise.'

'And your parents? How do they feel?'

'They don't know yet,' she was bound to confess. 'I plan on contacting them when we get to Crete.'

Christa raised an eyebrow. 'You're saying you didn't know before we sailed what Alexis had in mind?'

'Not altogether,' Zoe hedged.

The question came low, but with no less impact. 'Are you pregnant?'

Zoe could feel the heat rising under her skin. She attempted to infuse righteous indignation into her denial. 'No!'

It was difficult to tell whether Christa believed her or not. Zoe tried to tell herself that it was unimportant *what* she believed. Whatever the reasons for this marriage, it was her and Alexis's concern, no one else's.

The restaurant was well patronised, the hotel itself almost full. Business for the family had to be good. She said as much to Christa by way of changing the subject.

'Thanks to Alexis,' the other returned. 'He financed the extensions and improvements to raise the Apollon from "E" class to "C" some years ago, and enable Costas and Merope to become involved. Costas's only income before that was from fishing. My brother takes his family responsibilities very much to heart.'

Just how much, Zoe was only now beginning to realise. At least this part of the family showed appreciation. How the Theodorous back in Athens would react to the marriage announcement, she hated to think. It was going to cause a stir in most quarters, she supposed.

No point in worrying about it until she had to, anyway, she told herself resolutely. They had the best part of the cruise to come yet.

*   *   *

They sailed on the Friday morning after being persuaded to spend an extra night on the island. Zoe found it quite a wrench to say goodbye. The next time she saw these people she would be a Theodorou herself, she realised. There would be no chance of any of them getting to the wedding itself due to the season's demands.

'We can always visit with them again later in the year, if you wish,' Alexis suggested as they watched the land recede. 'After the season ends, perhaps.'

Another five months or so, Zoe calculated. 'A honeymoon?' she asked lightly, and felt his swift sideways glance.

'If we're to be married at all, I see no point in waiting that long.'

'If?' She said huskily, 'Are you beginning to have second thoughts?'

The answer was a moment or two in coming. When he did speak it was with reserve. 'I'm in no doubt. The question of when the marriage should take place will be decided when I meet with your parents.'

Not exactly a full-blown reassurance, she thought hollowly, but the best she was going to get. The only time she felt any sense of sureness in his regard was when she was in his arms—and that was purely sexual.

Between Santorini and Crete lay nothing but clear blue sea. Apart from a couple of inter-island ferries, and one or two caiques, they appeared to have the sea to themselves. Shortly after lunch they were adopted by a school of porpoise, and for about twenty minutes were able to enjoy watching the graceful creatures cutting through the bow waves like long, slim torpedoes.

The swimming-pool was hardly large enough to enable all the party to dive in at once, so they took it in relays. Alexis, Zoe was proud to see, had the best body of all the men. She couldn't keep herself from watching him covertly, oblivious to the fact that others might see her even if he didn't.

'If I had any doubts about the way you feel, I'd be convinced now,' murmured Christa amusedly at one point. 'You look as though you'd like to eat him up!'

Zoe blushed hotly, then gave a rueful little laugh. 'I didn't realise I was being so obvious.'

'Perhaps not to everyone,' replied the other, 'but I can remember being unable to take my eyes off David too. He doesn't have quite the same appearance now, of course, but the years have been fairly kind.'

'I'd say very,' Zoe returned, viewing the man in question as he hoisted himself from the water. 'He's a handsome man altogether.'

'It wasn't just his looks that drew me,' Christa confessed. 'It was the difference in him from my own countrymen. He listened to my opinions, treated me as an equal in intellect instead of a chattel fit only to share his bed and bear his children. In Greece, even today, a woman can sometimes still be very much a second-rate citizen to some men.'

'I'm sure Alexis doesn't see it that way,' Zoe protested.

'Not to the same degree, perhaps, but he'll always be the dominant partner in your marriage because that's the way he's made. Are you capable, do you think, of accepting that dominance?'

Zoe gave a light shrug. 'Time will tell.'

'Then I can only hope it tells of success.' Christa smiled at her sister as the latter returned to her lounger. 'Having fun?'

'Oh, yes!' The girl was full of vivacity. 'Are you not going to swim today, Zoe?'

'Too much lunch,' she claimed on a deliberately lazy note. 'I'll pass for now.'

'Then I'll take my turn,' said Christa.

Watching the Greek woman cross the few feet of deck to slide into the water, Zoe tried not to let what she had said cloud the day in any way. Alexis was dominant, yes, but far from the autocrat she had first thought him to be. She could handle it.

CHAPTER NINE

CRETE was abundant not only with history and archaeology, but also with wild flowers of almost every imaginable variety. At this time of year they even spread over beach and rock in carpets of pink and yellow and white.

As the biggest island, it was fitting, Zoe supposed, that the greatest Greek god, Zeus, should be said to have been born here. Greek mythology had fascinated her ever since her early schooldays when a supply teacher had decided to while away an afternoon recounting the legends of Belerophon and Pegasus, of Perseus and Andromeda, of Theseus, who had come to Crete to kill the dreaded Minotaur. Unfortunately, the story-teller had allowed his enthusiasm to run away with him, and was hurriedly dispatched to pastures new after one eleven-year-old reported to his parents that Hercules had impregnated the fifty daughters of a neighbouring king in one night!

She recounted the story over dinner on the Saturday evening, after spending the day visiting Knossos and Malia, drawing laughter all round.

'Quite a guy, this Hercules,' commented David on a note that made Zoe wonder if he regretted the lack of children of his own. She had taken for granted that he and Christa hadn't wanted to be tied down with a family, but it could well be otherwise.

There was no telling Christa's thoughts on the subject; she looked relaxed enough. Unlike last night, when they had gone ashore in Iraklion for dinner, they had stayed on board tonight.

Tomorrow they were to sail round to Agios Nicolaos, and from there head for Karpathos. Where after that, Zoe still wasn't sure. No doubt if she mentioned a particular desire to visit one or another island, Alexis would be only too pleased to indulge her, but she was content to just go along.

She had posted the letter telling her parents the news, and hoped it would have reached them by the time she got back to Athens. It hadn't been an easy letter to write, but, whichever way she put it, it was going to be a shock for them, so in the end she had simply said that she and Alexis had fallen in love and were going to be married, and that she would contact them more fully later.

The music coming through the speakers at present was of the easy-listening variety. Alexis made the first move to take advantage of the extra space created by covering up the pool, coming to draw Zoe to her feet.

Held close in the circle of his arms, she could feel the movements of his thighs through the thin silk of her dress, and knew a sudden rush of blood to the head. The eyes she turned up to him were deep, luminous pools, causing the arms about her to tense and his mouth to take on an answering sensuality.

'So the barriers are withdrawn,' he said softly.

He was too perceptive by half, Zoe reflected. Or was it just that she was too transparent? He was right, of course; she was physically receptive again. If there were any barriers left at all, they were only in her mind.

'It was foolish of me to allow you to be given the cabin next to Sofia's,' he added. 'I think tonight you must come to me instead.'

'I can't do that,' she protested. 'Someone might see me!'

'If you mean the crew, it's no business of theirs.'

'Perhaps not, but I'd still be embarrassed.'

'And that means more to you than being with me?'

She looked at him helplessly, not at all sure of his mood. 'I *want* to be with you, Alexis. You can't doubt that!'

'But it's the man's place to come to the woman, yes?'

'Well, yes, I suppose so.'

'I see. You want equality in all things except for those you find not to your taste.'

The heavy irony in his tone triggered anger in her. 'It has nothing to do with equality! Apart from anything else, we might not be as lucky again.'

'You think I would have failed to take account of that possibility myself?' he asked. 'Better that care be taken until we're safely married, yes, but don't expect me to live the life of a celibate between times.'

Looking into the dark eyes, she felt her anger give way. She had her love to keep *her* warm between times. 'I wouldn't expect it,' she said quietly, 'any more than I'd want it for myself. Only I can't do what you're asking and come to your cabin, and you can't come to mine because of Sofia, so it seems we'll both have to contain ourselves for the duration of the cruise.'

It was difficult to tell his reaction to that statement from his expression, but his voice had a distinct edge to it. 'So it appears. In which case, you'll do me the kindness of not tempting me the way you were doing a few moments ago.'

The accusation was not without foundation, Zoe acknowledged ruefully. The problem lay in damping down her emotions to a point where they could be contained. There was another week or more to go before they could be assured of any kind of real privacy. Large and roomy though she was, the *Hestia* was simply not the place for clandestine meetings.

If any of the others were aware of the dissension between them, they gave no sign of it. Back at the dinner table, Zoe sat twisting her wine-glass between her fingers as she listened with half an ear to the general conversation. Sofia looked so happy and carefree. Her life was opening up, her horizons widening. Christa deserved the main credit for that. For the rest, no blame could be attached.

There was another private yacht moored some short distance away. Little more than fifty feet in length, she seemed to be carrying about the same number of passengers, to judge from the noise they were creating. At least a couple of the men were English, Zoe knew, having been afforded wolf-whistles and a shouted invitation to visit when she had ventured up alone on the sun-deck prior to leaving for Knossos that morning. A charter party, in all probability, Alexis had declared on first sight, with a disparaging look at the vessel's shabby paintwork. One or two of the minor companies ran their businesses on shoe-strings.

He was pleasant enough to her, if somewhat distant, during the rest of the evening. Zoe danced with David and with each of the other two men, chatted desultorily with the women, and waited for the time when she could plausibly plead tiredness and take her leave.

It was gone twelve-thirty before she felt able to do so. Sofia elected to join her, but the rest of them looked set for the whole night.

'It's been such an enjoyable day!' declared the younger girl with satisfaction as the two of them made their way below. 'The very first time I ever visited Knossos, I'm ashamed to say!' She winged a fond glance. 'I've done so many new things since you came, Zoe!'

'And many more to come,' promised the latter recklessly. 'There's no reason why you shouldn't come too when Alexis and I go to England. I'd love for my parents to meet you.'

'I think,' came the doubtful reply, 'that Alexis may not consider it a very good idea until he himself has met them.'

'So? Christa and David will be returning home. You could always stay with them while we go up to Warwick.'

'So I could.' Sofia looked suddenly hopeful. 'I would love to come!' They had reached her cabin door. She added tentatively, 'Will your parents expect that the wedding should take place in England?'

'I don't know,' Zoe admitted. 'I suppose it would depend on how much time they were given to arrange things. Is it likely to cause problems if they do?'

'None that couldn't be corrected by a second ceremony here, I should think. Like many others, we attend church infrequently, as you know, but marriage within it would be looked upon as very important.'

Zoe groaned inwardly. Something else to worry about! Aloud she said, 'I'm sure Alexis will have it all in hand.'

It was going to be necessary to discuss the matter, she thought when she was alone at last in her cabin. Standing there in the darkness, she felt an unbridled longing to be in Alexis's arms. When he held her and kissed her nothing else seemed important.

Her bedside clock was showing twenty minutes past one when she finally heard the others coming down to their respective cabins. By a quarter to two the only sound still to be heard was the gentle slapping of water against the hull. She waited another fifteen minutes before sliding her feet from the bed to reach for her Paisley-print wrap. Going to Alexis now after all she had said was tantamount to submission, but she no longer cared. All she did care about was being there.

There was someone still on the bridge, she realised, hearing a cough as she reached the upper deck. She hugged the superstructure on her way forward. The owner's state-room was in darkness, but the bulkhead door was unlocked. Zoe slipped silently inside, closing it again and standing for a moment while her eyes adjusted themselves after the bright moonlight.

The sudden movement as Alexis lifted himself up in the bed made her throat go dry. 'It's me,' she whispered.

He didn't switch on a light to her relief, but simply threw back the covering sheet. His voice was low, a caress in itself. 'Come.'

She slipped off her wrap before joining him. His arms welcomed her, wrapping her close as he kissed her with a passion that roused her to swift and eager response. The thin straps of her nightdress slid down easily. Naked to the waist, she arched in ecstasy beneath the marauding mouth.

There was a hot, melting sensation between her thighs, a desperate craving for that full and powerful penetration. She could barely hold herself in check while he peeled the clinging material down the length of her legs, kissing him feverishly as she opened herself to him.

He entered her forcefully, but no more so than she was ready for, thrusting hard and deep with an urgency echoed by her own. Her heartbeats drummed like thunder in her ears, drowning out the sounds torn from the depths of her throat. Then she was over the top and floating, drifting weightless in utter peace and contentment.

'Why did you change your mind?' Alexis asked softly some unknown time later. 'I thought you were afraid of being seen.'

Zoe stirred in his arms, only now beginning to acknowledge that she could hardly stay here all night. Voice husky, she said, 'Discretion goes out of the window when desire comes in at the door.'

His laugh was low. 'It's good to know that I exert such an irresistible pull.'

Say it, a voice inside her urged. Tell him how you really feel. But the words weren't ready to come. Not yet.

'You're a wonderful lover, Alexis,' she said instead.

Even with eyes adjusted, it was difficult to see anything beyond the darkness in his. 'How would you know? You have no other experience to judge by.'

'I've read enough and heard enough to know that not all men are capable of giving that much pleasure to a woman.' She reached up to touch his face, allowed her forefinger to follow the line of his cheekbone down to the corner of his mouth, belly fluttering as he turned his head a little to trap the fingertip between his lips. 'The only reason that some wives plead headaches as a way of escape has to be because they don't enjoy their husband's lovemaking all that much.'

'So if you tell me you have a headache yourself some time I'll know what you really mean,' he said with his lips against her palm.

The delicate flick of his tongue on the sensitive inner skin was pure stimulation. Zoe felt desire mounting in her again, the delicious, spine-tingling excitement coursing through her veins. Not for Alexis the one-time satisfaction; he was too virile, too potent for that.

Not the same overwhelming passion either, but a quieter, deliberated arousal that made her tremble all over in anticipation as he kissed his way along the tender underside of her arm to reach the curve of her breast and enclose her nipple in his mouth, caressing it gently at first with lips and tongue, teasing it into aching prominence before commencing an erotic, rhythmic sucking that turned her molten inside.

She lost all sense of time and place and knew only the feel of his hands and lips moving over her body so intimately. There was no last inch of her that he left untouched, no place that he hadn't kissed and caressed and made free with.

He entered her slowly, oh, so slowly this time, holding himself back to extract the maximum pleasure for them both. It was, Zoe thought euphorically, in the suspended moment before he began to move again, the most exquisite feeling in the world to be so wholly and utterly merged with the man she loved. She wanted to stay there for all time, secure in his possession—a wish soon forgotten as the surge carried her up and away to a world where nothing else existed but sensation.

Drifting again afterwards, she came suddenly wide awake as realisation dawned. Alexis raised his head to look at her questioningly.

'What is it?'

'We . . . you didn't take precautions,' she got out.

'I was too intent to remember,' he acknowledged. 'Although I believe there's little danger of conception just now.' His tone revealed no particular concern. 'I find it difficult to consider precaution when you come to me the way you did tonight.'

'Then I'll have to stay away,' she said.

He rolled away from her suddenly to lie on his back, a forearm thrown across his forehead. When he spoke again it was brusquely. 'There are times when I think you have no desire for children at all!'

'That's not true!' She was rigid with resentment at the unfairness of the accusation. 'I just don't want to be halfway to having one before we get round to legalising the position—*if* we ever do.'

His voice came low and harsh. 'Are you saying there's doubt still in your mind?'

'Lots.' Zoe was sitting up, arms hugging her knees in an effort to counter the sudden chill in the air. 'All we have to hold us together is...this. I'm not sure it's going to be enough.'

'It will have to be enough. The announcement has already been made.'

'It can be unmade.' Zoe was aware of saying things she hadn't intended to say, hadn't even thought of saying, but couldn't seem to stop saying. 'I'm sure they'd all agree that mistakes are better rectified sooner rather than later. The question of marriage never entered your head before the possibility of my being pregnant arose—any more than it entered mine.'

'But it's there now, and there it stays,' Alexis returned hardly. 'I won't allow——'

'*You* won't allow!' Her voice shook with the swift, searing fury. 'I have a mind of my own, in case you hadn't noticed!'

'A very changeable one.' He came upright himself, the anger blazing from him. 'Why did you come here to me now if it was your intention to withdraw from our arrangement?'

Her shrug was defensive. 'As I've told you in the past, women are just as capable as men of being carried away by passion. Anyway, I didn't say it was my intention. All I *am* saying is that we should perhaps give it a little more thought.'

'I stand by my word. I expect you to stand by yours.' All trace of the tender lover had vanished. 'What must I do to convince you?'

Tell her he loved her, Zoe thought numbly. Only that wasn't going to happen.

He made no move to stop her as she slid from the bed. She drew on her wrap with fingers that felt stiff. Her nightdress was somewhere, but she couldn't bring herself to look for it. Only a short time ago she had been in heaven. Why, oh, why couldn't she just accept things the way they were? Half a loaf was better than none at all.

She left the state-room without another glance in Alexis's direction. He was lying down again—perhaps already asleep. The wind had stiffened during the last hour or so. It flattened the cotton wrap to her legs. The skies too were clouded over. Captain Dimitris had mentioned the possibility of a storm, though he predicted a short duration.

The other yacht had gone, she was surprised to see as she moved aft. It had been there an hour ago, for certain. It seemed a strange time to sail, but then what did she know about such matters? The way she felt at the moment, the subject was of little interest.

The storm broke around four o'clock, although here in harbour it caused the minimum of discomfort. Zoe got about an hour's sleep, all told. She rose at seven-thirty feeling anything but refreshed, to hear that although the worst of the weather had passed over the seas were still too rough to venture forth on the next leg of the cruise for at least another couple of hours.

'Apparently it blew up worse than forecast, although it was fairly short-lived,' said David. 'Glad we weren't out there in it! Does anyone have any idea what time the other boat left?'

'Two-thirty, according to Dimitris,' supplied Alexis. His eyes met Zoe's fleetingly and expressionlessly. 'I wasn't aware of it myself.'

'I went out like a light too,' agreed the other man. 'I wonder what possessed them to sail at that hour?'

Alexis shrugged. 'Possibly the hope of beating the storm to their next port of call.'

'Might they have managed it?' asked Zoe, drawn despite herself.

'Not to any of the other islands in the time. Heading north, the nearest is Thira; east would be Kassos and Karpathos. Either way, they'd be out in open water when the storm struck them.' He considered her thoughtfully. 'Why such concern?'

Zoe lifted her shoulders. 'Fellow-feeling, I suppose. There were some English people on board.'

'*All* English,' supplied Christa. 'And all of them men—although they appeared to have brought some girls aboard last night. Hopefully, they put them ashore again before they sailed.'

David was looking at her with interest. 'How come you know so much about it?'

She laughed. 'I was invited to join their party myself when I took a walk along the quayside while you were dressing for dinner. I would, I was assured, have a great deal more fun with them than here on the *Hestia* with my own dull menfolk. It was suggested that I bring along the gorgeous redhead too, which led me to believe that I was perhaps but a means to an end.' The last with a smile in Zoe's direction. 'They were certainly more your age group than mine!'

Unlike David, Alexis obviously found the tale far from amusing. He looked, Zoe thought, positively grim. She hoped he didn't believe that she had offered any encouragement.

Christa expressed regret to her later for passing on the story to him.

'I tend to forget,' she said ruefully, 'just how proud and possessive my countrymen can be. The thought of some stranger speaking of you with such familiarity wouldn't be pleasing to Alexis. It's probably a good thing that they did leave. Otherwise he might have felt honour-bound to go and effect retribution.'

Zoe could imagine. Alexis's pride was all-important to him. Anyway, they were unlikely to be seeing the other boat again.

They finally sailed at eleven, giving Agios Nikolaos a miss to head directly for Karpathos. Apart from the broken cloud cover still hanging over Crete itself, the sky was as blue as ever. The wind was down to little more than a stiff breeze, but the waves were still running higher than Zoe had experienced before. The motion, once they left the shelter of the land, caused a queasiness which she fought a losing battle to suppress.

She was lying on her bed when the call came for lunch. Sofia came down some minutes later to find her, and was mortified to discover her condition.

'I thought you simply wished to be alone for a while,' she apologised. 'I didn't realise you were ill!'

'I'll be OK if I just lie here,' Zoe assured her weakly. 'I couldn't eat anything.'

'I'll go and tell Alexis,' said the other girl decisively.

She was gone before Zoe could draw breath to protest. Bare moments later, or so it seemed, Alexis himself arrived. He had brought some tablets with him, and went to get a glass of the ship's purified water from the bathroom.

'You should have had these before we left harbour,' he said, handing her the glass as she raised herself up a little, and sitting on the edge of the bed to hold out the tablets on the palm of his hand for her to take one at a time. 'Prevention is better than cure. They may take a little time to work.'

Providing they stayed down at all, Zoe reflected, subsiding again. At the moment it was touch and go.

The wave of nausea ebbed, but it would return, she knew. She wished Alexis would go. It was bad enough feeling like death without having him see her looking like it.

'You might feel better if you came up on deck,' he said. 'The movement down here at water level is far more pronounced.'

Zoe shook her head, and immediately wished she hadn't. 'I'd rather just lie here until it passes,' she murmured. 'I just need to be left alone.'

'As you prefer, of course.' He sounded abrupt again. 'Try and get some sleep.'

She felt worse when he'd gone, both physically and emotionally. She lay there in a welter of self-pity until sheer exhaustion finally claimed her.

The bedside clock was showing ten minutes to four when she opened her eyes again. Tentatively lifting her head, she found that the nausea had gone. The movement of the boat was different. Only when she sat up and listened did she realise that the engines had stopped, although there was plenty of activity on deck.

Getting cautiously to her feet, she stood for a moment to adjust her balance before padding across to the port. A few hundred yards away lay another yacht—the same one that had left Iraklion in the early hours, she was fairly sure. It was also at a standstill, though facing in the opposite direction. A dinghy with three people on board was just leaving the other vessel and heading this way.

Needing a shower and change of clothing before even thinking of venturing on deck, she stayed at the port to watch the dinghy's approach. The two male passengers she recognised as the same ones who had gesticulated at her the previous evening. They appeared to have luggage with them too. Only when the boat had disappeared round the stern, to reach the boarding gangway on the starboard side, did she make a move, curiosity running rife.

Showered and refreshed, she brushed out her wet hair and left it to dry naturally, then put on clean white shorts and a simple vest top that left her arms and neck bare. More of a Titian than a true redhead, she had never found any difficulty in acquiring a tan, and was now a smooth golden colour on all exposed parts. She both looked and *felt* healthy at the moment, she thought thankfully, and hoped that the nausea wouldn't return when they got under way again. The sea certainly seemed much calmer than it had been earlier.

They were moving once more by the time she was ready. She found everyone gathered in the saloon, along with the two newcomers. Of them all, it was Alexis who appeared the least pleased to see her.

He introduced the pair as Greg Newton and Mark Beasley from London, and explained briefly that their own craft had developed engine trouble and was putting back to Iraklion to make repairs.

'She's only managing about four or five knots on the one engine, so it's going to take her a long time to make port again,' supplied the one named Greg when it seemed evident that his host was going to say no more. 'The others flew in scheduled, so they can get their tickets exchanged and fly out from Crete, but we're on a charter flight from Rhodes tomorrow afternoon. We're hoping to pick up another lift from Karpathos in time to make it.'

Owing to their late start, they wouldn't reach Karpathos before seven this evening, Zoe reckoned, which left the two of them on a pretty tight schedule. It seemed odd that people who could afford to hire a fifty-foot yacht for a holiday, even in conjunction with others, should be flying charter to start with. They were both in their mid-twenties, and wearing the common garb of denims and T-shirt, which gave little idea of their status.

'We got a deal on the yacht through one of the other guys who's in the travel business,' said Mark, as if reading her mind. 'A real tub compared with this, of course.' There was a begrudging note in his voice. 'Some of us have to work for a living.'

Alexis was close enough to hear the remark, though he showed no reaction. Greg had the grace to look a bit embarrassed.

'It was good of you to stop and take us off,' he said hastily. 'We tried to get a ferry to pick us up earlier, but no go.'

'They have a timetable to keep,' came the clipped reply. 'The storm will have caused enough of a disruption without non-essential delay. If I'd known the actual nature of the assistance requested myself I might not have felt inclined to render it either. In no way could it be classed as an emergency.'

Having faced that withering disdain herself on occasion, Zoe could feel empathy with the young man. She smiled at him. 'Good luck with *your* timetable, anyway.'

He smiled back, open admiration in his eyes. 'Thanks.'

There seemed little inclination on the part of the others to offer the usual easy Greek hospitality to the pair. Taking their cue from Alexis's attitude, Zoe gathered. While appreciating that it been wrong to signal an emergency in such circumstances, she couldn't bring herself to leave them sitting there in semi-isolation while she obeyed the same unspoken mandate. They were, after all, her own countrymen.

'What do the two of you do for a living?' she asked, more for something to say than through any real desire to know.

'We're both in computer operations,' Greg acknowledged. 'Same company.'

'And the rest of the party you were with? Are they in computers too?'

'Only one of them. The others have various jobs. We all met up on a Club Med holiday last year,' he added, pre-empting her next question. 'As Mark said, the yacht idea for this year came through one of the guys who's with a travel agency. We plan on doing something similar next year too.'

'It must sound like small potatoes to you,' put in Mark on a deprecatory note, 'when you're used to all this!'

'I'm not,' Zoe denied. 'I was no more born to "all this", as you call it, then you were. I come from a very ordinary home in Warwick.'

Greg said curiously, 'So how did you get to be here with all these Greeks?'

Alexis had moved off in response to a query from David, and was engaged in conversation. Zoe opted for a half-truth. 'I'm employed as a companion to the girl over there,' she replied, indicating Sofia, who was talking with the other women.

'Some job!' Mark sounded scarcely less antagonistic. 'They don't treat you like an employee.'

'No,' she agreed. 'When do you have to be back at work yourselves?'

'Nine sharp, Tuesday morning, or risk finding ourselves on the redundancy list,' said Greg. 'That's why we resorted to desperate measures. Jobs aren't all that easy to come by just now. We were due to turn the yacht over tomorrow morning, so the plan was to get to Rhodes tonight. Leaving when we did, we'd have made it easily, storm or no storm, if the engine hadn't quit on us. I suppose we were lucky they didn't both go. It was pretty rough for a while.'

'I'm glad we weren't in the thick of it,' Zoe commented with feeling. 'I found it more than rough enough at eleven when we sailed.'

'How long will you be staying at Karpathos?' asked Mark.

'Just overnight, I think,' she said.

'And then where to?'

'Rhodes.' She saw the expression which sprang in his eyes, and wished she had feigned ignorance. Even if

Alexis was willing to take them along, and that in itself was doubtful, they wouldn't be there so very much sooner than the ferry. 'I believe there's an inter-island air service,' she added. 'I shouldn't think they fly at night, but you might be able to get a flight in the morning.'

'With about three thousand drachmas between us, and Visa cards already over the limit, that idea's out of the window for starters,' came the tart response. 'We're cleaned out till next month. That's the way the other half lives!'

'Leave it out, will you?' Greg himself was beginning to sound a bit weary of the acrimony. 'We'll get there somehow—even if we have to stow away! The flight isn't until six o'clock.'

'Wouldn't your friends have made you a loan?' ventured Zoe.

'They did,' he said. 'All they could scrape together on the spur of the moment. There aren't many banks at sea.'

There wasn't very much she could say to that, Zoe conceded. Nothing much that she wanted to say. She had enough problems of her own without taking on anyone else's.

She stole a glance in Alexis's direction, heart heavy at the thought that this time yesterday they had been together, not alienated the way they were now. Her own fault, of course. She wanted too much. After what she had said to him last night, there was every chance that she might finish up with nothing at all.

CHAPTER TEN

SLOPING up from the harbour, Karpathos town lay to one side of a broad sandy bay. The sun was already disappearing behind the skyline of mountains, the red roofs taking on a darker hue as evening moved towards night.

Pighadia, home-town of Poseidon, the sea god, Zoe recalled, standing at the rail as they came into port. The northern part of the island had been cut off from the outside world until a few years ago, and the islanders there were said still to preserve their traditional way of life. She would have loved to see it for herself, but if they were only here for this one night it was impossible.

'Not exactly bustling,' commented Greg, at her side, viewing the general scene. 'I'd say we're going to have trouble picking up that ride to Rhodes in time to be of any use.' He slanted a glance when she failed to reply. 'You wouldn't consider doing us a big favour, I suppose?'

'That's a negative question,' she parried.

'A negative answer too, I'll bet,' said Mark shortly. 'We're on our own, mate!'

Zoe only wished she were on *her* own right now. The last couple of hours had been far from relaxing. Alexis had made no attempt whatsoever to break up their little trio, and she had found it difficult to do so herself. And now this request. There was no mistaking what they were after. The trouble was that she couldn't help feeling some sympathy for their predicament, self-inflicted though it undoubtedly was. The kind of holiday this group of theirs had chosen to take just couldn't be done on a shoe-string, deal or no deal.

'I'm not in a position to make any promises,' she said with reluctance, 'but if you genuinely can't find anyone else to take you I suppose I could ask. I'm not sure what time we're supposed to be leaving, though. It could still be too late.'

'Worth a try.' Greg sounded relieved. 'You're one in a million, Zoe!'

Or the biggest fool out, she thought wryly. She could only hope that they would find other means of transportation. The way things were at present between her and Alexis, she doubted if he'd be prepared to indulge her in any request, much less one concerning these two. He had made his opinion of them plain enough.

Whatever his opinion, he paid them the courtesy of coming out on deck to see them off when the *Hestia* was berthed and the gangway run down. Zoe was relieved that no mention of her offer was made. With any luck, Alexis need never know about it.

'Are we staying on board for dinner?' she asked when the two men had disembarked.

'I know of a taverna in Aperi where they do a very special *arnaki exohiko,*' he said. 'We can be there in fifteen minutes by taxi.' He paused. 'Unless you'd prefer to remain here, where your friends can find you again?'

Zoe kept her tone neutral. 'They can hardly be called friends.'

'But you obviously found their company more agreeable than that you've been forced to suffer these past days.'

Her hands, curved over the rail, showed white at the knuckles. 'That's unfair!'

'Is it? You showed no inclination to retire to your cabin while *they* were on board.'

'I didn't feel ill any more.' She made a supreme effort to keep control of her emotions. 'I stayed with them only out of politeness. Would you have had me just leave them sitting there on their own, the way everyone else seemed to be doing?'

'They were very fortunate,' Alexis clipped, 'that I allowed them to stay on board at all after I realised that the emergency was no such thing. Treat them as welcome guests, I would not! And yes, I expected you to hold them in equal contempt after I told you how they came to be here, not to smile on them approvingly!'

'It wasn't approvingly,' Zoe denied. 'It was——' She broke off, shaking her head in unhappy recognition of her inability to make him understand. 'It's unimportant.' She forced herself to look round at him, standing there in hard-edged profile, and braced herself to say what she so desperately wanted to say. 'Alexis, about last night——'

'So far as I'm concerned, the commitment still exists,' he interrupted brusquely. 'I told you that then, I tell you again now.' He straightened away from the rail, the eyes he turned on her devoid of expression. 'The decision in the end has to be yours.'

Half a loaf or none at all, the choice was still the same, Zoe thought hollowly as he moved off. Telling him she loved him wasn't going to make any difference.

She went below instead of following him back to the saloon, and spent the next hour or so trying to convince herself that this marriage of theirs could work, given a chance, but without very much success.

At eight-thirty, no nearer a conclusion, she took another shower and put on white cotton trousers and the little apricot blouse which she hadn't worn since the visit to the Plaka so many aeons ago, slid her feet into white leather mules. Viewing herself in the mirror before going up to join the rest of the party for drinks on the after-deck, she made a mental comparison with Leda Kazantzi's appearance, and doubted if she could ever achieve the same degree of style—or self-confidence either, for that matter. Leda might not love Alexis to quite the same depth, but she would make him a far more suitable wife. He must surely realise that for himself.

The others were dressed casually too, as they had been for most of this cruise so far. Rhodes was rather more cosmopolitan than the other islands they had visited, Zoe understood. Alexis had acquaintances there, which would probably mean more people to meet.

Laughing over some remark of Christa's, he looked so very different from the man she had left on deck earlier. Prolonged ill-humour was alien to the Greek psyche. She couldn't give him up, Zoe thought achingly. The mere idea of never seeing him again, of never hearing his voice or feeling the strength of his arms about her was unbearable.

They travelled in two taxis over the headland to Aperi. Fringed by olive groves, and with no less than three sandy beaches, it was in the process of becoming a popular resort for tourists, Zoe gathered from the amount of people already there. Alexis was greeted with joyful familiarity by the proprietor of the taverna he had spoken of—a welcome extended to the whole party as tables were pushed together and extra chairs found to accommodate them.

Sofia drew immediate and openly admiring attention from a group of young men occupying a neighbouring table. She pretended not to notice, but the sparkle in her eyes and bubbling animation was indicative that she was enjoying the experience. Wearing virginal white, with her dark hair floating free about her lovely face, she was enough to turn any man's head, Zoe thought. She certainly merited better than Orestes Antoniou.

The spiced lamb was every bit as good as promised. Greek cuisine might not be the best in the world, but *at* its best, Zoe considered, it had a lot of merit. Dancing began, some of it Greek, some modern, all of it energetic. Surprisingly Alexis made no objection when one of the young men next door came and asked Sofia to dance. She was, Zoe supposed, safe enough, and obviously not averse to the idea.

'Were you really considering Orestes as a husband for her?' she asked the man seated at her side, watching the pair as they circled past.

The shrug was light. 'There was never any question of compulsion, although she might do worse.'

'She could do a whole lot better, too.'

'By waiting for a man she can truly love to appear?' There was irony in his smile. 'She may wait a long time. Emotion of that kind is a luxury, not a necessity.'

A luxury she couldn't afford to hold out for herself, Zoe acknowledged with resignation. 'I think you might be right,' she said, and felt his swift glance.

'Does that mean you have no more doubts?'

The others were engaged in conversations of their own and unlikely to overhear anything they were saying. All the same, Zoe kept her voice low. 'It means I'm prepared to put them aside, if you're sure it's what you want?'

'My resolution was never in question,' Alexis responded levelly. 'Would you like some more wine?'

'Please.' She watched the lean fingers as he topped up her glass, cherishing the memory of their possessive power. No going back on it now. She was fully committed. For better or for worse.

Sofia returned to the table looking on top of the world. A moment or two later she was up again as another of the Greek youths claimed her. Zoe would have preferred to remain sitting out, but found it difficult to refuse when David asked her to dance with him.

'Is everything OK with you two?' he asked candidly when they were on the crowded floor. 'Christa thought you both looked a bit strained earlier.'

'A misunderstanding, that's all,' she said.

'Over those two idiots this afternoon?' He shook his head. 'They'd a damned nerve putting that one across! You can't blame Alexis for feeling the way he did.'

'I don't,' Zoe responded. 'But they were a bit desperate.'

'Their own fault for cutting things so fine—timewise *and* financially. No provision for eventualities.'

'Spoken like a banker,' she teased lightly. 'Anyway, they're probably well on their way to Rhodes by now.'

'Only if they found someone willing to take them for nothing, which is unlikely. I've a feeling we haven't seen the last of them yet. Not that I imagine Alexis is going to be prepared to do them any more favours.' He paused, looking down at her with speculation in his eyes. 'You know, I still find it hard to take in. Alexis never seemed the type to let his heart rule his head.'

'It can happen to anyone,' Zoe said on the same light note. 'As with you and Christa, for instance. One look, and you were lost!'

'True.' He was smiling at the memory. 'Except that I was quite a piece younger than Alexis at the time. Still, he obviously knows his own mind.'

And follows his own uncompromising rules, Zoe could have added. In no way did it involve the heart.

There was no sign of Greg and Mark when they returned to the *Hestia* in the early hours, much to her relief. After what David had said, she had more than half expected them to be waiting on the quayside.

Alexis kissed her continental-style on each cheek by way of saying goodnight, leaving her yearning for the previous night's passion. The temptation to go to him again later was almost overwhelming; she had to make a concentrated effort to control it. If he had wanted her with him he would surely have given her some indication. Better if they both got a good night's sleep.

Morning dawned bright and cloudless, with a light breeze to blow away any lingering cobwebs. Later in the year, Zoe knew from past experience, the *meltemi* could whip up a strength that would make last night's squall seem trifling. Boats could be confined to port for days on end, and tempers frayed by the constant buffeting, but right now all was harmony.

The brilliant clarity of light to be found down here in the islands was breath-taking. Drinking coffee on the after-deck, Zoe felt that she could stay there all day, just soaking up the radiance. The waterfront was a hive of activity, with fishing-boats unloading their morning catch and people thronging to make their choices from the glistening, gleaming trays before they were carted off to market. Noise ebbed and flowed like the tide.

'I don't suppose Rhodes is anything like this?' she said to Christa, who was nearest to her.

'I think you'll find the old town picturesque enough,' the other responded. 'Although it's many years since I last visited the island myself; so much might have changed.'

Standing at the rail, legs tautly muscled beneath well-fitting white shorts, Alexis had his back to them, but was close enough to overhear.

'You'd perhaps prefer to give Rhodes a miss and continue on to Kos or Kalimnos?' he asked on an odd note without turning his head.

'Not at all,' Zoe denied. 'How long is it likely to take us to get there?'

'That,' he said, 'is dependent on how fast or slow we go.' He swung to look at her, eyes narrowed, mouth clamped. 'Your friends from yesterday are approaching. Did you invite them?'

A mixture of guilt and sheer dismay brought a hot flush to her cheeks. She bit her lip. 'Not exactly invite,' she said. 'They asked me if I'd ask you, should they be unable to find other means of getting to Rhodes. I found it difficult to say no outright. I'd hoped they'd be gone by now.'

'I see.' His tone was clipped. 'So you had better ask me, had you not?'

In anger, his English became more formal, Zoe noted irrelevantly, not for the first time: each word so cold and precise. She could appreciate his attitude, after all both he and David had said, but it was a little too late to try telling him that.

'All right, I'm asking you,' she said instead, trying to keep her tone easy. 'Will you take them, please? Their flight is at six o'clock.'

He remained where he was for a lengthy moment, eyes boring into her, then he jerkily inclined his head and went forward.

'I guessed they'd be back,' commented David unnecessarily. 'In fact, I'd be willing to bet they never even tried to find any other means of transport. You should have given them the elbow right away, Zoe.'

'I know,' she acknowledged unhappily. 'I'm just not that hard. It isn't really such a big deal when you come to think about it. A few hours, and they'll be on a plane for home.'

'Making it imperative that we leave Karpathos right away,' said Christa on a note that drew Zoe's gaze her way in sudden doubt.

'Wasn't that the plan anyway?'

'Originally, perhaps. Alexis was saying before you came on deck that we should take the opportunity to sail up the coast to Diafani and visit Olympos. He thought you might like a glimpse of the real traditional Greece.'

Zoe bit her lip. It was exactly what she would have loved to do. No one else made any comment. They didn't need to. She had deprived them all of an experience that might not come their way again, and for what?

Alexis returned with Greg and Mark in tow, both of them looking as if they'd spent a rough night. Whatever his feelings on the subject, Alexis was putting a good face on it, Zoe conceded, as he offered the pair coffee. Of the two, only Greg revealed any hint of discomfiture. The glance he sent Zoe's way was apologetic.

They left harbour some fifteen minutes later. As the rest of the party dispersed to various points, Zoe was forced to the conclusion that as the invitation had been hers it was going to be up to her to entertain their new passengers over the coming six hours or so. Sofia had deserted her too, whether at Alexis's instigation or her own, there was no way of knowing.

'Unfriendly lot, aren't they?' observed Mark sourly when the three of them had the after-deck to themselves. 'Talk about being made to feel welcome!'

'Considering you're getting a free ride, I don't think you've a lot to complain about,' Zoe responded tautly, not about to let *that* pass. 'You're only here at all because I made the mistake of opening my mouth too far!'

'Is that a fact?' He studied her with insolent interest. 'You must have more pull than you made out yesterday.'

'It wasn't pull that got you on board,' she denied. 'Just Greek chivalry. Alexis wouldn't embarrass me by refusing to take you after I'd more or less issued the invitation.'

'Alexis, is it?' The insolence increased. 'Seems they're friendly enough with their employees—or are you a special case?'

'Will you cut it?' Greg was angry. 'You've been like a bear with a sore head since we left Crete! So that girl you brought on board didn't put out. Tough! You don't have to take it out on every other one you meet.'

'Why not?' came the curt retort. 'They're all the same. I wouldn't mind betting this companion thing is just a cover-up.' His eyes hadn't left Zoe's face, registering her heightened colour with a knowing expression. 'What kind of a salary does it pay?'

If ever there was a time for clarification, that time was now, but something in Zoe rebelled against doing it. She owed this upstart no explanations.

She said coolly, 'A very good one. And I might point out that we're still a lot closer to Karpathos then we are to Rhodes, so if you don't want me to go and suggest turning round again I think you'd better shut up.'

Mouth set in a sneering little smile, he gave a shrug. 'Sure.'

Zoe got up from her chair and went to the rail to cool off. If she'd had the strength, she would have thought nothing of tossing that crass idiot back there overboard with her own hands! It was people like him who gave the English a bad name abroad.

Greg joined her, leaving his friend lounging back in apparent unconcern. 'Sorry,' he offered gruffly. 'I feel rotten about this. I don't know what's got into him.'

'You mean he's not usually so bitter and twisted?' she said without turning her head.

'Not to such an extent. I suppose it might have something to do with all this. It's the way he'd like to live himself.' He gave a laugh. 'The way we'd all like to live!'

'There's nothing wrong with a little envy,' Zoe rejoined, 'providing it stays rational.' She added with purpose, 'There's an old saying, trite but true, about cutting your cloth according to your means. I think you both bit off a bit too much with this cruise business, don't you?'

'More than a bit,' Greg agreed wryly. 'A case of trying to keep up with the pack. The others make more than we do. We've put ourselves in hock for months because we neither of us had the guts to say it was out of our pockets in the first place. If we don't make that flight, we're completely stuck.'

'Surely you'd have been able to wire your families, or something?' Zoe ventured.

'For what good it would have done. My folks have trouble keeping their own heads above water. If my father knew what I'd spent on this trip he'd throw a blue fit! It's near enough as much as he makes in six months.'

'Well,' she said lamely, 'at least you've got the experience to look back on.'

'I suppose so. It was a pretty good fortnight, I don't mind admitting.' He put a hand on her shoulder. 'Thanks, anyway. I don't know what we'd have done without you.'

Alexis was on the sun-deck above; Zoe had heard his voice just a moment ago. It was unlikely that he would be looking down here, she told herself, resisting the urge to move away. Greg was simply expressing gratitude, nothing more personal.

'You'd have managed,' she said lightly. 'We should be there by three. That should give you plenty of time to get to the airport.' She searched her mind for something else to say. 'Where did you stay last night?'

'We camped out on the beach,' he admitted. 'Not the best bed I've sampled, but it could have been worse.' He moved the hand still resting on her shoulder in a gentle caress. 'How long are you here for?'

'No set period,' she prevaricated. She wished now that she'd told the truth from the start. It had been idiotic of her to conceal her status. She murmured softly, 'Don't do that, please.'

Greg took the hand away with reluctance. 'Sorry.'

'You don't have to be,' she said, trying not to make too much of it. 'Shall we go and find a drink, or something?'

'Sounds good,' he agreed.

Zoe waited for some comment from Mark when she turned away from the rail again, but he just gave her a dirty look. There was no way he was going to relinquish his role, that was obvious. Just so long as he kept his opinions to himself from here on in.

The pool was uncovered, the water slapping gently back and forth in tune with the movement of the yacht. Greg eyed it longingly.

'My trunks are right at the top of my bag,' he said. 'Do you think anybody would mind if I had a dip?'

'Feel free,' invited Alexis shortly from above, and they turned as one to see him looking down on them from the sun-deck. 'You can change in the saloon,' he added. 'It's unoccupied at present.'

Which meant that the rest of the party were up there with him, Zoe surmised. She felt isolated. Angry though Alexis had every right to be over this unwanted intrusion, he had no cause to treat her like a pariah! The hurt roused her to an anger of her own. If that was the way he wanted it, so be it!

'I'll join you,' she said to Greg with deliberate familiarity. 'Ten minutes.'

Down in her cabin, she searched out the gold-coloured suit she had bought on impulse yet never yet dared to wear in the open. Cut almost to the waist on the leg, it plunged equally low at the neck. Studying herself in the mirror, she knew a momentary doubt, swiftly crushed beneath a fresh surge of resentment. She'd show Alexis how little she cared for his ostracism!

The young crewman named Adonis was coming along the alleyway as she emerged from her cabin. The flimsy wrap she had donned over the suit swung open as she turned, eliciting a look of unstinted admiration in the bold dark eyes.

'*Oreo!*' he declared, followed by something else under his breath. '*S'agapo, despinis!*' he added extravagantly. '*S'agapo!*'

Zoe summoned a smile, taking him no more seriously than he meant to be taken. If Alexis could only say, 'I love you,' to her, nothing else would matter. But he didn't. Not in any way she cared about.

Greg was already in the water. Arms propped on the side, he let out a slow whistle as she approached. 'That,' he declared, 'is what I'd call a sight for sore eyes!'

'Shark-bait,' muttered Mark, obviously determined to stay in character.

Without looking up, Zoe had no idea whether they were under observation from the upper deck or not. The rancour that had got her into the suit was already beginning to give way to regret. The whole gesture smacked of nothing so much as a childish desire to shock. She could imagine the contemptuous curl of Alexis's lips at the sight of her, not just because of the display itself but because he would know why she had done it. Too late now to turn back, of course. She had to see it through to the bitter end.

The last thing she felt like doing at the moment was swimming, but there wasn't much else for it. She dived in cleanly, surfacing to find Greg right in front of her.

'You've got it all!' he said. 'Looks, figure, ability— the lot. Why couldn't I have met you back home?'

'It obviously wasn't fated,' she responded lightly. 'It's pure chance that we met up at all.'

'But you're not out here for good, are you?' he insisted. 'How long is this job of yours supposed to be for?'

It was time, Zoe acknowledged ruefully, that she came clean. It had been stupid of her in the first place to allow the misconception. 'There's something I should tell you,' she said. 'I'm not——'

'Zoe!' Alexis was standing in the saloon doorway, face set in lines that tautened every muscle in her body. 'I wish to speak with you.'

She gave Greg an apologetic little smile, then swam the few strokes across to the ladder, pulling herself from the water with reluctance. If the suit had left little to the imagination before, it must leave even less now in its sleek wetness.

The few yards of deck she had to cross seemed to stretch forever. Alexis raked her from head to foot with a look in his eyes that mortified her, then turned back into the saloon in a clear indication that she should follow him.

'The master calls,' said Mark tauntingly as she passed his chair. 'Time to pay your dues, is it?'

Zoe ignored him. In another few hours he would be out of her life altogether. She was concerned only with the here and now.

Alexis had taken the spiral stairway leading from the saloon to the lower deck. She followed him down, and along the alley to her cabin. He held the door open for her to precede him, the tautness about his mouth a warning of what was to come.

'Take it off,' he gritted when they were both inside with the door closed again. 'Now!'

Zoe caught her lower lip between her teeth. 'Alexis——'

'I said take it off,' he repeated grimly. 'Unless you wish me to strip it from you myself!'

She sighed and gave in, turning towards the bathroom.

'Not there, *here*,' he said, halting her in her tracks. He indicated the white towelling robe which she had left on the bed. 'Put that on instead.'

'You're just trying to humiliate me,' she protested, and saw his lips twist.

'You already humiliated yourself by displaying your body for those two out there to gape at! No Greek woman of class would consider making such a spectacle of herself!'

Both words and tone cut to the quick, arousing a fierce backlash. 'But I'm not Greek, and I'll wear what I damned well please!' she spat at him. 'If you don't like it, you know what you can do!'

The glitter in his eyes became a blaze, frightening in its intensity. 'I know *exactly* what I can do,' came the dangerously soft response.

He had reached her before she could make a move, stripping the wet suit from her with a ruthlessness that left no option, tearing it down the front before tossing it aside to regard her with fury still burning bright.

'You'll learn to respect me,' he said, 'even if you have no respect for yourself!'

There was a total lack of gentleness in both hands and mouth. Zoe fought like a tigress to escape the punishing kiss, but it was impossible to break free of him. She had no defence against the hard caresses. There was a moment when she thought he was going to go further, then he put her forcibly from him to seize the robe from the bed and hold it out to her.

'Cover yourself,' he said harshly.

Zoe drew the robe on and belted it securely about her waist. She felt degraded, not just by Alexis himself but by her own conduct.

'I'm sorry about the suit,' she forced out. 'I should never have bought it, much less worn it.'

'Had you worn it when the two of us were alone, that would have been a different matter,' came the curt response. 'You'll stay below now until we dock and those two are gone.'

If he had asked, or even suggested that it might be best, she would probably have gone along with it, but the peremptory command aroused instant contention, jutting her chin and bringing a fresh spark to her eyes.

'I don't think so. I invited them, so they're my responsibility.' She added with purpose, 'We English must stick together!'

A shutter seemed to come down over the hard-boned features, blanking out all expression. 'If that's the way you feel, perhaps you might prefer to accompany the two of them back to your own country? It can easily be arranged.'

How had it come to this? Zoe wondered numbly, even as pride dictated her response. 'Why not? I'll start packing. You can send the rest of my things on when you get back to Athens.'

She turned away from him jerkily, afraid that she might give way. It was over; there could be no going back from here. Alexis had seized on the excuse to get rid of her too readily for it to be anything but what he really wanted.

The cabin's outer door closed in his wake as she reached the bathroom. He would have gone to tell the others, she surmised. A man of swift and implacable decision, was Alexis Theodorou. Well, she could be decisive too. A clean break was best all round. It would never have worked out anyway. There were too many differences between them.

It took her little more than fifteen minutes to pack. Although it wasn't yet midday, she put on a skirt and blouse after showering and drying her hair, so that she wouldn't need to come down and change again later. She moved in a kind of emotional limbo, feeling nothing but a dull depression.

Eventually, knowing she had to face them all some time, Zoe made her way up top. Greg and Mark still had the aft-deck to themselves. Fully dressed again, the former eyed her curiously.

'You were gone so long, I decided to call it a day,' he said.

'One or two things I had to do,' Zoe replied on as casual a note as she could manage.

'I'll bet!' Mark kept his voice low, but the tone spoke volumes.

It was a bit too late now to put him in his place, Zoe acknowledged without caring overmuch. He was going to have quite a surprise when he realised that she was to accompany the two of them to the airport. In the meantime, he was at liberty to think what he liked.

Greg made no further overtures, but seemed content just to lie and bask in the sun. If nothing else, he remarked, he would have a good tan to show off at the office. Zoe made a pretence of reading the paperback novel she had left lying around for a couple of days, even remembering to turn the pages occasionally, although she didn't take in a solitary word. Occasionally she was aware of being under observation from the sundeck, but she didn't lift her head to see who was there. Lunchtime would be soon enough for confrontation.

Except that no one seemed inclined towards comment either by word or by glance when the time came. Alexis himself appeared, on the face of it, to have forgotten all about the morning's episode, although he avoided any direct communication with Greg and Mark, Zoe noted. She looked away whenever he happened to glance in her direction. If their eyes once met, he might see something in hers that she didn't want him to see.

They made Mandraki Harbour just before three o'clock, sailing between the twin pillars once bestraddled by Colossus. Standing at the rail, Zoe readied herself at Alexis's approach, but couldn't bring herself to turn her head and look him in the face.

'I'm all ready to go,' she said. 'The three of us can share a taxi to the airport, so you don't need to concern yourself any further.'

'You,' came the oddly muted response, 'are going nowhere. Not before we discuss matters more thoroughly, at least.'

The others were mostly over on the starboard side, watching the docking procedure. It was just the two of them. Zoe said thickly, 'What good is that going to do?'

'I'm not sure,' he replied. 'But we have to try and find a way to make things right between us again.'

'They never have been right.' Her throat ached with the effort of keeping her voice steady. 'It was a mistake from the beginning. We both know that. We're two people at total odds with each other, Alexis. You want the kind of woman I just can't become.'

'And you?' he asked softly. 'What is it that *you* want?'

What was the use in pretending any longer? Zoe asked herself. Why not just say it and have done?

'Love,' she answered. 'I know you see it as totally unnecessary, but I can't. If and when I marry, it has to be to a man who loves me back the same way. All you feel is a sense of obligation. It isn't enough.'

He hadn't moved, yet something in him had tensed; she could sense it. When he spoke his voice was roughened.

'You said, "loves me *back*". Does that mean what it appears to mean?'

'Yes, it does.' She made a wry gesture. 'And that places you under no obligation either.'

The gangway was being lowered. Greg and Mark would be ready to go. Alexis might have had second thoughts with regard to her leaving at the same time as the two of them, but she didn't think she could bear to go through it all again.

'It's better this way,' she said. 'Leda Kazantzi will make the ideal wife for you. I'll go and fetch my case up.'

He made no move to stop her. Zoe carefully avoided looking at him as she turned away. She made her way below, feeling absolutely numb from the neck up. It would start to hurt some time, she knew, but if she could just get through these next few hours...

Her suitcase was where she had left it by the bed. Hoisting it, she took a last look around the cabin that had been home for the past week. She could have had it all on a permanent basis if she had been willing to settle for less than the best. Only she wasn't. All, or nothing, that was the choice, and nothing was what she had.

She had left the door ajar. Turning to see Alexis standing there was a shock because she hadn't heard him coming along the alleyway.

'I could have managed,' she said, assuming that he had come for her suitcase. 'It isn't all that heavy.'

'You're not going anywhere,' he declared. 'Not unless I'm there too.' His voice thickened. '*S'agapo*, Zoe.'

Her heart leapt, then sank back into the trough. 'Saying it doesn't make it true,' she repudiated. 'I want the real thing, not some pretence!'

'There is no pretence.' He came all the way into the cabin and closed the door, then moved across to where she stood and took the suitcase from her unresisting hand to drop it back down by the bed. His hands came about her waist, drawing her towards him, then he was kissing her again, only this time there was no anger in him, just tenderness and warmth.

Zoe cast doubt aside as she responded. The whys and wherefores could wait. For now it was enough to simply be. She lost track of time and place as tenderness gave way to passion, warmth to heat. Desire was enhanced by love, reaching an intensity beyond anything she had known before.

It was some time before the world finally steadied enough to allow rational thought again. They were lying entwined on the bed, clothing scattered about them. Feeling her stir, Alexis lifted his head to look at her, his eyes deep and soft.

'So much misunderstanding,' he said. 'And all for want of a few words. I believed *I* was the only one to feel any depth of emotion.'

'And I thought I was so transparent,' Zoe murmured. She cupped his face between her palms, cherishing the strong, clean lines. 'How long have you known?'

'Since I discovered what you had given me. The very thought of another man knowing you the way I knew you was more than I could bear. My feelings for you outweighed all other considerations. If it took pregnancy to make you marry me, then I prayed for you to be pregnant. Anything rather than lose you.'

'How could you not know how I felt about you?' Zoe asked. 'Even Christa said I wore my heart on my sleeve where you were concerned.'

'Your attraction, perhaps. *That*, I could recognise. But, as you said yourself, a woman can be drawn to a man for purely sexual reasons, with no deeper emotion involved.' He paused, searching her face. 'You appear to be so much more at ease in the company of your own countrymen—even those who are strangers to you. First back in Athens with the young man you met so casually, and then again with these other two, you were a different person. In asking them to come back this morning, you made it seem that you yearned for your own kind.' His mouth twisted. 'Jealousy is a destructive emotion. It puts words in the mouth that were never meant to be spoken. When you agreed so readily to my suggestion that you accompany the two of them, I was devastated.'

'No more than I was myself.' She added softly, 'I've known jealousy too. Of Leda. She seems to me to be everything you could possibly need in a woman.'

'*You*,' he declared, 'are everything I both need *and* want in a woman.'

'But I'm not Greek.'

'As I am not English.' He paused again, his regard questioning. 'Can you truly be happy away from your home and people?'

'With you, yes,' she said. 'As Christa was with David. I dare say there'll be times at first when I feel a bit homesick, as I'm sure Christa did too, but I can visit, which she couldn't. I love your country, Alexis. And your people. I always have. It will be no hardship for me to make my home here.'

Eyes kindling, he kissed her long and possessively, arms wrapping her close. Zoe responded with elation in her heart for all that was still to come. Life with Alexis might not always be peaceful—he was too dominant a character for that—but it would never be dull. She had her very own Greek hero!

'You look radiant!' declared Christa with no perceptible trace of envy in her voice. 'Pregnancy really suits you.'

Zoe laughed. 'We aimed for another Easter baby, but the best-laid plans, et cetera ... Anyway, July is a good month, too. I'll be able to take her in the pool almost right away, the way I did with Andreas. He swims like a fish already.'

It was Christa's turn to smile. 'You're so sure it will be a girl?'

'Artemis is, and she's never wrong. We're going to call her Helen. No one with that name could fail to be anything but beautiful.'

'She would be anyway, with you and Alexis for parents.' Christa glanced across to where her brother sat talking with Zoe's father. 'Speaking of which, I'm happy to see your own here and looking so much at home.'

'So am I,' Zoe agreed. 'It wasn't easy for them to accept that I'd be living so far away, but we manage to visit, one way or the other, several times a year, so it isn't that bad. They're over the moon about the new baby, of course. Being the only surviving grandparents makes them doubly conscious of their status. I only hope Andreas isn't going to be jealous when he has to share their attention.'

'I doubt if he'll lose out,' said Christa drily, transferring her attention to the small group paying court to the dark-haired two-year-old birthday boy in their midst. 'Boys are always favoured above daughters.'

'Not in this family. Equality all the way down the line!'

Christa looked amused. 'You sound as if you might have had trouble claiming your own.'

'Still do,' Zoe admitted with humour. 'Alexis pays lip-service to the idea, but tends to ignore it when it comes to something he considers too important to be decided by a woman.'

'If you've survived three years, you'll survive the rest.' It was said with confidence. 'The way you two feel about each other, you'd be lost apart.'

So true, Zoe thought, her eyes on the man she had married. The occasional disagreements made no inroads on other, more vital emotions. They were as much in love now as on the day they married, and nothing was going to alter that.

Three years! It hardly seemed possible. Andreas had been born almost a year to the day after they first met. Alexis had expressed both joy and a certain relief on confirmation of her pregnancy. After two pre-marital failures, he had said only half jokingly, he had begun to doubt his ability to produce a child at all. Now, with their second one due in a couple of months, his *perifania* was fully restored.

Sofia caught her eye, winging a happy smile. She had been married a year now herself, to a man she loved and was loved by. So much worth waiting for, she had acknowledged more than once. Her first child was due in September, with three more to come, as she was fond of declaring. If she had ever possessed a travel urge, it wasn't in evidence at all these days. She was totally content with what she had.

As if sensing his wife's contemplations, Alexis looked across, dark eyes taking on that spark reserved for her alone. They'd do far more than just survive, Zoe thought with certitude, returning the look with love. They had a lifetime to come.

ATHENS—'the cradle of civilisation'

With a history that began 2,500 years ago in ancient times, Athens is a city which has always had romance at its heart. Today, visitors can see the city's glorious past living side by side with the cosmopolitan present. Famous classical landmarks rub shoulders with the hustle and bustle of modern life—in Greater Athens, you'll find two-thirds of Greece's motor vehicles!

THE ROMANTIC PAST...

Athens is based around two hills, the **Acropolis** and **Likavitos**. The **Acropolis**, with its marvellous views across the city, is one of the earliest settlements in Greece, dating from Neolithic times. The monuments which can be seen today date from the time in the fifth century BC when the Delphic Oracle ordered that the flat-topped hill become the home of the gods. Therefore, modern tourists will see temples and sanctuaries dedicated to such mythical figures as Athena and Artemis, though most come to view the **Parthenon**, which is called the centre of the ancient classical world. The building of the **Parthenon** was begun by Pericles, ruler of Greece, during a golden

183

age when the country had repelled invasion by the aggressive Persian empire, and philosophers such as Socrates and Plato were putting forward new ways of thinking. Therefore the **Parthenon**, which was a new sanctuary for the goddess Athena, completed in 437 BC, reflected this cultural supremacy in its architecture, which was in the *Doric* style.

At the foot of the **Acropolis**, visitors will also find the **Agora** which, as the market-place, was the heart of classical Athens; the buildings there represent the whole of Greece's golden period, being built in between the sixth century BC and the fifth century AD.

For lovers of antiquities and classical history, a visit to the **National Archaeological Museum** is a must. This imposing building houses one of the finest collections of ancient sculpture and bronzes, and pottery and ceramics, excavated throughout Greece.

THE ROMANTIC PRESENT—pastimes for lovers...

With its strong mythological and cultural heritage, Athens is an immensely civilised city, and so an ideal venue for romantics!

If you want to see modern Athenians going about their business, **Sintagma** or **Omonia Squares** are the places to be. **Sintagma**—or Constitution Square—is the city's principal square, being flanked by the parliament building (formerly the Royal Palace), luxury hotels, airline offices and banks. **Omonia** is equally as busy but also full of the bright lights, as it is the Athenian equivalent of London's Piccadilly Circus, or Times Square in New York.

But for those who prefer more peaceful surroundings, the beautiful **National Gardens**, next to **Sintagma**, are an oasis of calm—and the perfect meeting-place for lovers. Sub-tropical trees and statues provide cool shade in these gardens designed by Queen Amalia, and there are peacocks and ponds full of waterfowl. On spring evenings, you can even hear nightingales sing.

Perhaps the most romantic quarter of Athens is the **Plaka**, situated on the northern slope of the **Acropolis**, which is a charming and intriguing maze of white-washed houses in narrow streets, alleys and stairways. Here you will find the pulse of Athens' night-life, crammed into numerous bars, *tavernas* and *estiatorio* (more pricey restaurants).

Eating out in Athens, like the rest of Greece, is a special experience. It's not unusual in tavernas to visit the kitchen and choose your dishes. As in Italy, a Greek meal may start with a rice course, such as *piláfi sáltsa*, or pasta (*makarónia*), perhaps baked with minced meat or cheese, or with *hors d'oeuvre—taramasaláta*, for example, which is of course a paste made from the roes of the grey mullet fish blended with olive oil. Main courses will consist of meat or fish, perhaps *moussaká*, a traditional dish of minced beef, auber-gines, cheese and spices, or *souvlakia*, small kebabs of meat grilled on a skewer, or *tsoutsoukakia*, which are meatballs. Popular fish dishes are *barboúnia* (red mullet) and *kalamarákia* (baby squids).

Sweets are usually eaten separately, rather than as part of a meal, but are no less delicious; *baklava* is made up of layered pastry filled with nuts and honey, while *kataîfi* is wheat shredded and filled with sweetened nuts; *galaktobourenko* is pastry filled with vanilla custard.

Meals are most often accompanied by *salátes* (salads), perhaps *dománta* (tomato), and by cheese: *fetta*, a soft, white cheese of goat's milk is very popular. Food is washed down by a selection of wines: *retsina* is a resinated white wine—more popular in the countryside—or **Demestica** and **Amalia**, which are unresinated. Before a meal, the favourite Greek aperitif is *ouzo*, which is made from grape stems flavoured with aniseed.

No visit to Athens and the **Plaka** is complete without strolling through the **Flea Market**, which is to be found in the winding streets around **Monastiraki Square**. Though the market proper takes place on Sundays, the browser and the collector will find shops and stalls all through the week selling all kinds of items, like pottery, icons, leatherware and jewellery: it's best to make sure that you've plenty of **drachmas** (Greek currency) to spend!

Ending our whirlwind tour, **Piraeus** is the port of Athens—one of the busiest in the Mediterranean—and the gateway to the Greek islands, since ferries leave regularly for destinations that include the **Cyclades** (where you'll find the islands of **Kithnos, Naxos, Paros** and **Santorini**), **Aegina, Crete** and the **Dodecanese** (**Rhodes, Kos** and **Patnos**), although there are actually 1,425 islands altogether in Greek waters!

POSTCARDS FROM EUROPE

HARLEQUIN PRESENTS®

Travel across Europe in 1994 with Harlequin Presents. Collect a new Postcards From Europe title each month!

Don't miss
MASK OF DECEPTION
by Sara Wood
Harlequin Presents #1628

Available in February wherever Harlequin Presents books are sold.

Hi—
It's carnival time in Italy! The streets of Venice are filled with music—the costumes are incredible. And I can't wait to tell you about Lucenzo Salviati....
Love, Meredith

Relive the romance...
Harlequin and Silhouette
are proud to present

A program of collections of three complete novels by the most requested authors with the most requested themes. Be sure to look for one volume each month with three complete novels by top name authors.

In January: **WESTERN LOVING**   Susan Fox
                                        JoAnn Ross
                                        Barbara Kaye

Loving a cowboy is easy—taming him isn't!

In February: **LOVER, COME BACK!**   Diana Palmer
                                         Lisa Jackson
                                         Patricia Gardner Evans

It was over so long ago—yet now they're calling, "Lover, Come Back!"

In March: **TEMPERATURE RISING**   JoAnn Ross
                                          Tess Gerritsen
                                          Jacqueline Diamond

Falling in love—just what the doctor ordered!

Available at your favorite retail outlet.

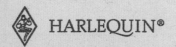